Looki
Mirror
You Can't Make This Up, Volume 1
Elunda Sanders
Published by GOD Publishing, 2024.

This is a work of fiction. Similarities to real people, places, or events are entirely coincidental.

LOOKING THRU THE MIRROR

First edition. June 14, 2024.

Copyright © 2024 Elunda Sanders.

Written by Elunda Sanders.

Dedication

Thank you for accompanying me on this insightful journey through the pages of this tale. I hope my words strike a chord with you, bringing the pages to life while touching your emotions. Gratitude is extended to those who grasp the hidden stories and connect themselves within these pages. Above all, to the struggle that God would not allow to defeat me!

Big shout-out to Brenda, Latisha, Linda, Felicia, Dawn, LeShaun! Just pulling your leg. May DMX rest in peace. Expressing heartfelt gratitude towards the incredible individuals – L. Grice, J. Hodges, A. Phillips, and B. Johnson - who have been an unwavering source of motivation and inspiration during this pivotal phase of my journey.

Chapter 1

In the Beginning, There Was Us

Like a moth to a flame, trauma and my life were intertwined in the womb, and my very existence was shaped by negativity. My mother and "father" raised me, together with my brother, Kyle, and sister, Candace, in the projects. My father, who was christened Tyrone, always commanded the room with an undeniable authority.

He was as tall as a beanstalk, had skin as smooth as silk, and a head of hair that was so top-notch that he could have been a model for shampoo commercials. Not to mention, he had enough military experience to make Rambo green with envy.

Dad treated his green Riviera like a precious gem, pampering it with turtle wax every Saturday. And as if that weren't enough, he would chauffeur us to the park, pushing us on the swings like a true superhero.

He was strict with us kids. He had a black belt, and I don't mean karate.

He was tough as nails and didn't hesitate to crack the whip on us. He appeared to adore us, but for some reason, my parents always treated me differently from my siblings. I was often in trouble and beaten for no apparent reason.

My mother was pretty as a picture, with a complexion as dark as night. She was a real head-turner, and her name was none other than Jennie-Mae. She was a real stickler for cleanliness, with a knack for making the laundry shine like nobody's business. My mother was a rebel with a cause, a story yet untold. Her spirit was wild and untamed. She upheld a fiery personality; let's face it, who needs central heating when you've got flames?

She drove a Malibu, and boy, did she have the pedal to the metal! She rode the winds of freedom. With every twist and turn, she conquered the open road. While she wasn't turtle waxing her car, she did take diligent care of it. You couldn't eat a piece of gum in that bitch.

They both had jealous tendencies, accusing each other of having affairs, and it felt like a battle was certain every Friday. We didn't have much, but we made do. My mom always kept our hair combed and our clothes immaculate, and it was hell to pay if we got dirty; ass beating central.

I was petite with long legs. My hair was as dark as a moonless night and cascaded down my shoulders like a waterfall. I was curvy in all the right places, with a goblet-shaped waist. I was equipped with a personality fizzier than a soda, a sunnier demeanor than a beach day, and a smile that could knock out a whole army of bad moods.

My smile was innocent at that time. However, I soon learned that every smile would later become a coping mechanism in the making. I had a nurturing nature. I always wanted to help, but I didn't realize that these attributes made me vulnerable to predators and would cost me dearly in the years to come.

My brother was two years under me, and my sister was two years younger than him. Although it was tough for us to make new friends, we always had each other. Kyle's ego was so massive you couldn't convince him he wasn't the hottest thing since sliced bread.

He strutted around like a Pretty Ricky wannabe with a head the size of a hot air balloon. He was more of a lover than a fighter, like a peaceful dove with an innate ability to avoid conflict. My brother had a talent for being a walking volume knob (loud) and a professional irrigator (obnoxious), but hey, at least he had some redeeming qualities, so nobody complained too much. My siblings fought like cats and dogs.

They could not get along to save their lives.

My sister, whose complexion could make a canary doubt its validity, possessed a shade of yellow that could cast doubt on the sun itself. She was an incredibly sassy dictator who insisted on being crowned queen of righteousness at all times. When it came to being her primary opponent, my brother was about as helpful as a houseplant in a boxing arena

By turning up the heat, Candice aimed to make his life a raging inferno. Even though she was barely out of toddlerism, her vocabulary was already impressive enough to embarrass a sailor. My mother must have had a cuss word radar because she always caught her red-handed.

The party was over when my mom shouted, Candace, "I'm going to beat y'all ass!" The one thing I knew was that if my parents promised us a beating, they would deliver without hesitation. So now it's up to me to act like a big sister and break up the fight. Even though they argued regularly, we maintained a close connection. I was the epitome of I AM MY SIBLING's KEEPER!

Our housing complex was decent. It was a neighborhood full of kids who spent a lot of time outside having fun. We didn't go out much, so school was the only place we met new people.

I loved the fall. Autumn was my favorite season. Going outside and watching the leaves change colors and eventually fall from the trees was one of autumn's greatest appeals for me. I always felt relaxed and at peace when I glared at the bright colors. However, all of that was cut short by pollen-induced sneezing. I frequently had puffy, watery eyes and a runny or congested nose.

My suffering was worth it for those elusive moments when my dad joined in on the fun, throwing my mom into a leafy abyss and commanding us to create a towering mound to conceal her. They were as rare as a unicorn sighting but worth the wait! Behind our seemingly flawless facade, we appeared to be a happy family. Once the curtains closed and the audience left, the real show began.

My parents were the life of the party, the social butterflies of the group. They had a tight-knit group of couples they partied with often, and they took turns hosting dinners, card games, and movie nights. We had to go along on a few occasions; it looked like they were having fun. However, as soon as we got into the car, they fabricated stories and made false charges about what had transpired during the party.

Plain stupidity. My dad would fire off with, "That nigga pulled the chair out for you; y'all must be sneaking around."

My mom would trigger back with, "Well, what was I supposed to say? No, thank you, my sorry-ass excuse of a man doesn't believe in chivalry. If you were so concerned, you should have done it." This exchange would go on the entire way home.

My parents were heavy weed smokers, so any gathering at their place looked like Cheech and Chong had thrown it. Because of my bad allergies, I always dreaded when they held parties at our place. By morning, I found it increasingly difficult to catch my breath.

Every time I mentioned this to my mother, she would angrily demand that I leave her alone and that I was exaggerating to get some attention. I don't know about you, but I can't fathom anybody lying about being unable to breathe. I could think of far more ways to seek some damn attention.

When I wasn't getting in trouble for silly stuff, I adored visiting my maternal grandparents' home, Jodi and Wilma. Grandpa Jodi was always there for my grandmother and the kids. Grandma Wilma never worked a day but managed to raise sixteen children; she was the disciplinarian of the family. She was heavyset, attractive, and had a harsh voice. She did not mince words; she said what she meant, and she meant what the fuck she said.

Granny would often discuss how she used to be an alcohol bootlegger and loved her children! I will tell you right now: no one in their right mind should mess with Mama Bear's cubs because she would get in the dirt with anybody. Grandma did, however, also have a softer side to her.

She was hilarious, loving, and clever in her remarks. I used to love hearing her sing. She would always sing this one phrase from one of her favorite hymns. "I come from a poor family. We didn't have much, but the Lord's been good to me."

My grandpa was an excellent instructor who could always find a lesson in any circumstance. The irony was that he had trouble reading. His mother died when he was incredibly young while giving birth, so he had no formal education. But he was a walking dictionary; he knew everything about everything, and you'd never believe he was illiterate. He had a gentle demeanor and rarely raised his voice, but he loved to drink.

He was amusing even when he was intoxicated. He'd pay us a dollar to dance, sing, or even fart. He always emphasized the importance of mastering a skill to show off our abilities. I admired him because he worked his ass off, refused handouts, and was willing to lend a helping hand or the shirt off his back for the sake of his family. But one thing was guaranteed: he would do anything to protect his family.

It's possible that my mom's parents were too cautious with me. I had a unique bond with my grandparents because of the fact my mother gave birth to me when she was a teenager while still living at home. Grandma Wilma treated me like her favorite granddaughter. My grandma always ensured I had an extra piece of watermelon because she knew how much I loved it. If I picked up the newspaper, she'd slip me a dollar, but the rest of my cousins were told to clean up and do as they were told.

My father's parents were divorced and moved on with new companions. My paternal grandmother, Julie, had eight children, all incredibly compassionate and loving qualities they were forced to inherit from her. Grandma's tongue was a double-edged sword; she never held back. She was honest and straightforward, so I had no problem trusting her. Best of all, I knew I had her undying affection whenever I was in her presence.

Grandma Julie's husband, Papa Richard, was a rigorous but kind soldier in the United States Army. I don't know much about their marriage, but I can tell you that he was an excellent grandfather. He always made time for us grandchildren, even after a full day at work.

He would tell us stories about his time in the army, which taught us discipline and compassion. Papa Richard wasn't just a soldier; he was a hero in my eyes. The complete opposite of my father's father, Jack.

Papa Jack reminded me of the uncle lurking in the shadows at the family barbeque, rubbing his hands together, licking his lips, waiting for any underage fast-ass girls to twerk or show up in their hottest come fuck me dress. Papa Jack was a man just like that! He often wanted me to sit on his lap, but it seemed like he always had a roll of quarters in his pocket.

Everyone constantly complimented us on how well-behaved we were when in the presence of others. We always appeared picture-perfect, but our picture was far from perfect. It felt like there was constantly a dispute or a battle going on. Domestic violence existed before it had a name in my family, but it wasn't your ordinary Ike and Tina type of shit; not only slapping on bitches but disrespectful degrading shit appeared normal.

My mother and her sisters were well-known in the town for jumping anyone who wanted smoke, and since ain't no rules in fighting, they had sticks, bricks, and all kinds of shits. It didn't matter to them if you were male or female; if you had problems, they were there to solve them. One of my uncles had the art of beating up bitch's down to a science as if he had graduated from whoop-a-hoe college.

My mother and her sisters were close and supportive of one another, even though they occasionally argued. They had nonstop phone conversations about everything under the sun. One day, my mother was talking with her sisters about a woman who had been sexually abused and beaten. "This is sickening all of this free pussy out here, and nigga's are raping people," my mother remarked.

What exactly does it mean to be raped, I wondered? Never in a million years did I think that being raped would become a defining moment in my life, much like the Kennedy family's "shot heard 'round the world." Unfortunately, the statement would come to characterize my existence. The sins of the father sometimes can become the child's reality!

When I initially heard the word, I had no idea what it meant, but subsequent exposure aroused my interest. My mother and aunt were talking about an incident. I overheard my mother explaining, "He led me to the woods near muddy water, and that's all I recall. I was so scared that I laced up my Nikes and took flight. My clothes were all ripped up and shit; all I was left with was a feeling of disgust. I told Daddy and Mama about it. Daddy got his shotgun and a bottle of Wild Irish Rose, and we went looking for his punk ass. I was afraid because he was psychotic, and I didn't want to go through the humiliation of a trial, so I let it go."

It was the second time that that word had drawn me in. I had to understand what it signified. Simply put, I needed to know what it meant, and the sooner I did, the better. I looked up the definition of rape. However, I was still unclear about the meaning, so I went to school the next day and asked Miss Stanforth what it meant.

The next thing I knew, I was speaking with a woman carrying a briefcase who was questioning me. She inquired about individuals touching me and began defining limits. She showed me some odd-ass images of a girl and a boy holding hands and described good and bad contact.

When I got home, DHS was at our house talking to my mother, and that was my first encounter with the expression, "You've got these white people all up in my business; you don't tell anybody anything that goes on in this house, and why would you ask such a thing, with your nosy ass."

I explained that I had overheard the conversation and wanted to know what it meant. It was months before I found out the true meaning. Unknowingly, I was fated to learn firsthand what that statement meant and how powerful the ramifications were, even after you were safe.

I recall it as if it were yesterday. I was eight years old, dressed in a Strawberry Shortcake T-shirt, blue jeans, and a left sock with a hole in the toe. The phone was ringing back-to-back. My mom and dad had gotten into it, so she wasn't answering.

Unfortunately, caller ID did not exist back then; only the element of surprise, like in a crackerjack box, you never know what you will get on the other end of that receiver. My mother picked up the phone and answered it, "YEAH! What? Oh, Hell No, I'm not going. I'll send her with her aunt and uncle. OK, I'll call you back when I finish cooking for these kids."

I was a curious child, not in the sense of being nosy about other people's business or gossip, but in the sense of being eager for knowledge, often misunderstood. It has followed me throughout my life. I wasn't interested in holding hands, kissing, or finding a boyfriend, and no, I was not fond of bitches; my focus was on knowledge and hustling. All I ever wanted to know was a little more. I've always been curious about why. Why things happened the way they did, and this unusual phone call was no exception.

Hmm, I wonder who was getting ousted out of the family. Was this my Last Supper? Hopefully, if it turns out to be me, I am entitled to some fine delectables before being kicked to the curb. I can imagine how Jesus felt in that upper room meeting; I was about to grasp a sense of betrayal, and I would never be the same. My mother and I went shopping the next day. Later that evening, my aunt and uncle picked me up. We went on a long car ride with a few of my favorite cousins.

When we arrived at our destination, everyone rushed to the car like they were greeting local celebrities, kissing and hugging me for some reason. I had never seen any of these people before. Many of them kept identifying themselves as my aunts and uncles, and this is your cousin such, and such. I am thinking, what in the hell is going on? Come on,

Chile, meet all the cats, dogs, and frogs.

The site was terrifying all in itself. It was a plantation with chickens, goats, and pigs running around the front yard. There must have been at least thirty people in this house, and when we awoke the following day, it appeared that everyone was sad; many were crying. I thought, "Damn, who pissed in y'all cheerios?" But the question remains: what is going on? Who are these people, and why am I here?

I didn't know what to make of it. Seeing a goat strung up in the backyard made me feel uneasy and ill at the site of its slit throat, and when my cousin, then 11 years old, took a chicken by the neck and rang it around, saying, "Watch this," he hacked off the head. The beheaded chicken then started to run amok. I let out a scream and bolted out of there. A few seconds later, the chicken appeared to be dead. After carrying it inside, he remarked, "Here goes breakfast." Suddenly, I had no appetite. *No thanks, I will pass.*

All of this made absolutely zero sense. The family train continued to roll as more individuals came through the door. This time, my uncle made the family introductions. "This is my sister; this is my brother." How could these folks be tied to me if they were my uncle's family? All right, the jokes are finished. Please tell me where I am and what's happening. My aunt was my mom's sister. Tyrone was my dad, so I couldn't possibly be related!

My aunt told us to wash up after breakfast. There were at least fifty people in there. When would we find the time to shower, and how would we choose who would go first? Do we take a number? Do we pick straws? How will all of this work? Ironically, they had an excellent little system. The kids went first, and since they owned four mobile homes in the area, each with two bathrooms, everything worked out.

My aunt got us all dressed. I remember wearing a beautiful yellow dress, socks with lace around the ankles, and patent leather black shoes. Someone curled my hair into Shirley Temple's locks. I don't think I'd ever felt so beautiful.

"It's time to go," my uncle said. My aunt packed us all into the car, and a caravan of about nine vehicles set out. As we wound our way down the twisting roads and past the sagging trees, I couldn't help but notice the unusual color of the dirt; it was red. I'd never seen anything like that before.

When we arrived, it was clear that the church had seen better days. I just knew the whole building would collapse in the event of a strong wind. The gloomy, dark chapel reflected the somber mood of the onlookers. The stench was disgusting. It smelled musky, aged, and shut in.

There was an open casket in front of the pulpit. A man who looked to be sleeping was inside. The man within the box confused me. I asked my older cousin, "Why is he sleeping in front of everyone?"

My cousin replied, "He is not sleeping, girl; he is dead." This was my first encounter with death. I had never been to a funeral before.

The scene was filled with deep emotion. A woman sitting in the front row was overcome with sadness. With a piercing gaze, her eyes focused on the casket, seemingly determined to see beyond its wooden exterior and connect with the cherished individual hidden inside. Her body trembled ever so slightly, a tangible reflection of the quiet sorrow that loomed over her. Next to her, a man sat with his head lowered, lost in contemplation or maybe defeat. His face displayed many emotions, with every line and crease telling a story of deep inner turmoil.

My uncle took my hand firmly, his voice barely above a whisper as he said, "Come with me." He led me through the crowd, our path winding towards the couple, the couple in the front row who subtly stood apart from the rest. As we neared them, my uncle leaned in, his voice soft yet carrying a weight of unspoken emotion. "Mama, here she is," he murmured as we approached the pair.

She squeezed me tightly and whispered, "I'm your grandmother, tell me your name." I was stunned into silence. All I could do was stare at her. The minister announced the services would start in five minutes.

The woman said, "Would you like to sit with me?" I declined with a shake of my head and followed my cousins back to the pew.

Before reaching the pew, my aunt grabbed my hand and drug me up to the casket, "Do you know who this is?"

I turned my head away from the coffin. "No," I replied.

"Look at him!" she exclaimed. I started feeling nauseous; my heart was racing so quickly that I couldn't breathe. It was getting harder and harder to ignore the pressure that had begun to build up behind my eyelids. I peered slowly inside the coffin as tears rolled down my cheeks.

She said, "This is your father."

Chapter 2

Blurred Images; Shattered Fragments

I felt like something from a scene from The Color Purple, "So, Pa is not Pa? Auntie, Tyrone is my father," I said, trying not to upset her while also assuring her that I was not retarded.

My aunt's words hung in the air, a weighty proclamation that left no room for doubt. 'He is not your biological father,' she declared, her voice ringing with a clarity that was as chilling as it was absolute. Despite sharing a home with your mother, he's not your father in the truest sense of the word; he's referred to as 'your dad,' a title not earned by blood but by virtue.

What in the Sam hell is she talking about? What in the entire fuck is virtue? A wave of emotion surged through me, threatening to pull me under. Tears welled up in my eyes, not for the lifeless body lying in the nearby casket, but for a different kind of loss. The tears were born out of a deep-seated fear of the unknown, a fear lurking in the shadows of my heart, now thrust into the harsh light of reality by my aunt's revelation.

Caught in a whirlwind of unfamiliar faces, I was utterly disoriented, a stranger in a strange land. The circumstances that led me to this predicament were as mysterious as the people's identities surrounding me. My mind, clouded with confusion, could only grasp one clear thought: I needed to return home. The urgency of my situation left no room for understanding or comprehension of my surroundings. My sole mission, my only beacon in this bewildering maze, was to find a way back to the familiarity of home. At least I knew what to expect there: chaos and commotion.

Never had I ever heard something so insane. Either your father is your father, or he isn't. Although I may not have understood everything happening, I was certainly old enough to grasp the notion that I had been bamboozled.

Numerous things were racing through my mind. The most crucial factor was my identity: who am I? Who are my actual kin folks? Will my communication with my biological father's family end here? Do I have an obligation to build a relationship with the new people in my life? Even more pressing, would my mom allow it?

Given my colorful history with my stepfather's family, I couldn't help but wonder what new surprises lay ahead. I was terrified of venturing into the unknown. However, I was still intrigued about how my relationship with my stepfather's family might develop.

Do I have to call them something else? Will I remain the apple of their eye, or have I turned rotten due to learning the truth? If the objection of affection is located within the secret place of the heart, the answers to these perplexing questions will eventually become apparent.

My grandparents, Papa Richard and Grandma Julie, were two of the most amazing things in my life. Will they remain in existence?

Whatever the future had in store, I was unprepared to face it.

After the funeral, I tried to fade into the background as much as possible, but the news that had just come to me continued to resurface into my head. What made my mother think telling me lies was a good idea?

I thought it would be a peaceful getaway from the stresses at home, but it turned out to be the most bizarre and surprising journey of my life, with more twists and turns than any back roads Mississippi had to offer.

Despite the valiant efforts of the kind-hearted individuals around me, my unmistakable unhappiness was as conspicuous as a peacock in a penguin parade. Despite my unparalleled confidence, I suddenly found myself in an emotional pickle. Trying to strike up a conversation, my grandma asked me what my favorite food was. I said, "Hands down, watermelon."

With a voice as vibrant as a rainbow, she remarked, "Chile, let's go for a stroll." My nervousness increased with every step we took. I felt as jumpy as a kangaroo on a caffeine binge. I was scared to death; the yard had turned into a full-blown animal kingdom right before my eyes.

Seeing the obvious concern in my eyes, my newfound grandmother extended a calming hand of direction. In a gentle voice, full of empathy, she stated, "Baby, you gotta act like you belong here; if you don't bother them, they won't bother you." *I don't belong here, so how the hell can I do that??*

The garden was bursting at the seams with produce. She suggested, "Pick a watermelon. I bet you've never seen one like this before." When we arrived inside, she cut it open, and I noticed it was yellow. She was not wrong. I had never seen or tasted anything so sweet.

Despite the fact that he was the youngest, I could see she adored my father. She unleashed a symphony of melodramatics in a whirlwind of emotions, exclaiming, "My baby, no, not my baby." Each wail pierced my heart like a thousand tiny arrows. I couldn't begin to comprehend her anguish. After a while, she became comfortable enough to show me some photos from my father's album.

Among the many images, one photograph stood out to me from the sea of others. Pictured with two little boys, like a trio of mischievous magicians, the photo drew me in; this one stole the spotlight.

When I questioned who the boys were, she casually dropped yet another bombshell: they happened to be my brothers. I asked whether they were there, and she nonchalantly shrugged her shoulders, claiming they couldn't make it.

Thank the lucky stars for the bell. Out of the blue, my cousin asked me to join her outside. I was chomping at the bit to comfort my grandma through her agony, but I was scratching my head on how to take the edge off her pain.

    Attempting to comprehend these new revelations had confused me more than a GPS in a corn maze. I was utterly disoriented; my signal had faded. Still, I'm just a young whipper snapper, so let someone else handle it. *Sorry, Granny, I am out of here!*

    My younger relatives had the duty of feeding the animals. They asked whether we wanted to feed the piglets and milk the cows. I want no part of it, no way. The others came over to get the slop meant for the pigs. As I was crossing the field, I heard something that sounded like an animal in distress. Of course, I was still afraid, but compassion drew me in.

    Upon closer inspection, I noticed a small pig was hurt; its hoof was jammed into the fence. I mustered the courage to liberate its leg. The pig squealed, and a gush of blood spurted out. Suddenly, my cousins started yelling, "Run, run!"

    Well, well, well, the hog jumped to conclusions and thought I was responsible for the piglet's mishap. I realized why my cousins chose to serenade me with their lovely chorus of "Run, run!" Porky Pig was in hot pursuit of my luscious loins. I dashed like a gazelle towards the open gate's welcoming embrace, barely avoiding capture.

    The grown-ups found it hilarious and couldn't resist capturing the moment on film for generations to come. Oh, the irony! While I trembled in fear, they were on the verge of splitting their sides from laughter. Classic! The Comedy Express had left the damn station, and I was clearly not on board. That took the cake! *So long, my country cousins! I want out of here!*

    The clock was ticking, and I was dead tired. We were hitting the road bright and early the following day. I only wanted to catch some Z's and sleep through the rest of it. Despite everyone's friendly demeanor, I couldn't shake this uneasy feeling that something fishy was happening.

I felt like a square peg in a round hole; I simply didn't fit in.

With the arrival of the new day, we indulged in a delicious breakfast, where the enticing smell of freshly brewed coffee blended harmoniously with the buttery fragrance of pastries. With our hunger satisfied and enthusiasm soaring, we made our final preparations before setting off on our adventure along the highway. As we embarked on parting ways, my grandmother gave me a warm hug and expressed her wish to stay in touch.

"Thank you for the watermelon," "I hope you feel better soon after losing your baby son," I said with a smile, trying to bring light to the situation. Our gazes locked, revealing a blend of sorrow and unwavering resolve within her eyes.

"That was not just my son we're talking about," she corrected gently, her voice barely audible; tears began streaming down her face. "That was your father, and don't let anyone try to convince you otherwise. You only have one father, and his name was Wayne! I've got something for you," she showed me two watermelons and told my uncle to put them in the car for me to take home.

As we drove down the highway, I knew I was returning to my new reality. With everything happening so fast, I tried to pause, look at the made-up pictures I was now faced with, picture myself in the unique setting, and wonder what new lies I would find.

My puzzled expression matched the overall theme of my existence. My mind was all jumbled up, like a jigsaw puzzle. What to do with this disorganized mess of pieces is beyond me.

I was trapped in a whirlwind of thoughts, each one playing on a relentless loop. The question that echoed loudest was one of identity: who was I, truly? Was my family defined by blood or by the bonds we forged? Would I ever hear from my biological father's family again, or was this the end of our connection? Is it my duty to build bridges with these new individuals who have suddenly appeared in my life? The most pressing concern is how to arrange all the bull shit logically.

Imagine the subsequent identity crisis. I have no idea who I am; the folks I've been looking at every day now appear to be as strange as the man in the coffin. I don't think anyone took the time to anticipate the impact this could have on me as a child. They didn't think it was vital for me to have a relationship with this man before he died, so why was it so crucial after he dropped dead? What purpose was this news going to serve?

To be honest about the situation, it really messed me up. Consequently, this was the start of my broken spirit. Everything that was anything appeared to be my fault from then on out.

We arrived back late on Sunday night. My siblings were delighted to see me when I stepped through the door. I was happy to see them, but would you believe neither of the adults in my life said anything to me? These two chuckleheads functioned as if nothing was going on. I wanted to ask questions, but where would I start?

A fuzzy picture can become apparent if you stare at it long enough. Although I may not have been the cause of the issue, I always seemed to be at its core. My parents may have seen me as the thorn in their perfect rose bush family photo, which included two fair-skinned children, a white picket fence, and debuting yours truly as the black sheep. I was confident of one thing: I felt like a stranger.

Exhausted from being bombarded with mind-boggling revelations and feeling as low as a limbo stick, I decided to cleanse my weary soul with a refreshing shower before surrendering to the cozy embrace of my fluffy bed. The entire sequence of events began to replay after I was in bed. It was simple to make the distinction; I now saw why I always seemed to get the shitty end of the stick. Bluntly, if I may, I was not Tyrone's child. I had a lot of questions and needed help figuring out where to turn for answers. I couldn't wait to get to school and tell my friends about this poppycock.

I had three close friends. We had been down since ponytails and royal crown hair grease, and they were the one constant in my life. Bianca, Tonae, Jessie and I all went to the same school. We used to walk and laugh together, throwing snowballs in the winter and running through water in the summer, but primarily, the only time I played with them was at school.

Bianca was as tall and slender as a supermodel. Bianca's smile could light up a room like a supernova, radiating passion and cheerfulness. Her eyes were like windows to a soul with more depth than the Mona Lisa. Back in the day, her mom rocked Hella barrettes on her ponytails. She was the Venus and Serena of our generation, serving up style and sass with every hair flip.

Tonae' stood tall, her knees bowed, which she emphasized by throwing her body around, or switching, as we called it, with a figure that could give a Coca-Cola bottle a run for its money. She was a force to be reckoned with, like a hurricane in stilettos. Whenever we managed to escape the watchful eyes of our parents, she would roll up her shirt and create a flawlessly disheveled bun, complete with strands of hair that seemed to defy the rules of gravity, framing her face in an act of rebellious elegance.

Of course, the boys couldn't resist their urge to tease, poking fun at her petite bosom and claiming she was a proud member of the 'ittybitty titty committee.' But Tonae couldn't care less about their juvenile remarks. She exuded confidence and had no qualms about telling those little rascals to pucker up and kiss her ass.

Jessie was a scrawny, bright, dookie, stain-colored youngster with a nappy head, who developed into a brilliant adolescent still nappy headed, nonetheless. He was a real loose cannon, always eager to let the chips fall where they may. But beneath the surface, he was a wolf in sheep's clothing. His heart was pure as gold, which clashed with his untamed nature. He always went above and beyond and showed the highest regard for other people. He was like my knight in shining armor!

Jessie was a real go-getter, constantly thinking of new ways to earn money. He'd run every idea by me, and I would tweak the plot until the schemes became a reality and the hustling era was born! We wanted to work but were too young, so we hustled by any means necessary.

We were strong-willed, like-minded kids, so effective collaboration was second nature. We became close as siblings as a result of our mothers' friendship, and because he was easy to talk to, I trusted him with all my secrets.

Bianca and I were the closest. Even though I couldn't come out to play, Bianca and Tonae would come up to my window, give candies, and talk through the window. That gesture provided the foundation and defined my friendship expectations. We were young girls who had no genuine concept of friendship, but that relationship set the tone. If you can't make it to me, fuck that, I'm coming to you; anything I have, you have.

Jessie would always come and get me, and we would walk to meet the others. I was hesitant to tell him about my new reality, but I gave it straight, no sugar coating. My thoughts have always been that when you put sugar on shit, it turns into sweet shit, and there was nothing sweet about this shit. Jessie was sympathetic and encouraging; he promised me that he would never tell anyone, which he didn't. I was so embarrassed that I cried.

Parents are often unaware that what you learn early in life formalizes and determines how you will live your life. These three were loyal, supportive, and giving; I mirrored those same qualities. We always had each other's backs. Even though I felt connected to Tonae and Bianca, and we were close, I couldn't tell them because I was afraid, they would make fun of me or use it against me later, as everyone else did. I had no idea who was genuine and who wasn't; I was lost.

Days later, I started asking my mother whether I had any siblings I didn't know about, and she said no, even though I did. I inquired about what my real father was like; she said, "Aside from being a horrible mother fucker, I have no clue about his character; he was a sick son of a bitch who raped me." Don't waste your time asking me any further questions about it." However, it truly bothered me. The more I attempted to put it out of my mind, the stronger my curiosity grew.

Each time I reflected on the situation, I experienced increasing physical discomfort, including severe nausea and frequent episodes of vomiting. It became evident to me that I suffered from intense panic attacks, although it seemed challenging for others to comprehend my condition thoroughly. After experiencing the same symptoms for two additional days, I noticed a change in my speaking ability. Despite my best efforts, I could not utter a single word, which caused me significant concern.

When my mother asked me to get the mail, I did so immediately. She asked me if I had seen her friend's car parked nearby; I shook my head no and returned to my room. After a short while, my mother came in and inquired about the discussion I had with my grandmother about my father.

I gave a shoulder shrug. She answered, "You got to know something." I just looked at her, thinking that although her answers to my questions were to get out of her face and leave her the fuck alone, it was interesting that she was now looking for answers. I was glad I was silent at that precise moment because I could have expressed my frustration in a less-than-ideal way.

I gazed upwards and let the waterworks flow, utterly perplexed about my inability to speak. No matter the outcome, I was convinced it would inevitably be my fault, and I'd find myself in hot water. Just when I thought things couldn't get any worse, my mom gave me a forceful whack to the back and screamed, "Need a reason to cry? I've got plenty!" and started hitting me until I fell to the floor and balled up.

The next day's events unfolded similarly. Unfortunately, it never occurred to me to leave a note explaining my inability to communicate, which she mistook for defiance. Of course, she complained about me to her sister.

"Jennie Mae, you need to take her to the hospital; she might be in shock," my aunt added. She agreed, which surprised me. The doctor explained to my mother that he couldn't promise anything, but most patients were back to normal within a few days. When she asked about the disorder, the doctor told her it was PTSD.

I saw her glaring in my direction; I closed my eyes and pretended I was asleep until I fell asleep. The following day, a speech therapist arrived and instructed me to perform a series of exercises; however, my ability to speak remained impaired. After a while, my mother placed the phone to my ear, and I heard my grandmother Wilma say, "Pray

Chile," which I did.

I kept repeating in my head. "God, please heal me; I'm at a loss for words; please help me." My voice was raspy the next day, but I could speak.

Choosing to turn a blind eye to the whole dad situation was my new game plan. Who in their right mind would sign up for another round of The Silence game? It was like a roller coaster from hell without the thrill. The doctor, channeling his inner Sherlock Holmes, started digging for the root cause. He thought it might be tied to some traumatic event and turned to my mom, asking if any skeletons in our family closet might be haunting me.

Without hesitation, she shot back a 'no' so firm that it could have knocked the wind out of a tornado. Then she gave me a sharp look as if challenging me to challenge her. Thanks, but no thanks. I got way bigger fish to fry, so I looked away.

Perhaps it was a stroke of genius that I kept my trap shut; otherwise, I'd have spilled the beans right down to the secret stash of her 'special herbs,' aka weed, tucked away in the top drawer! She couldn't care less about my well-being, so why should I lose sleep over it? My lips were sealed tighter than a gambler's wallet after a losing streak.

In my book, Tyrone would always be 'Dad,' a constant in a world of variables until someone else discovered the truth: he was merely a placeholder, a bookmark in an untold tale of deception. Until then, I'd be as silent as the tomb where my so-called father rested.

I realized that whatever answers I needed going forward, I wasn't going to get them from her, so I tried to bury the situation as best I could. Still, every time Tyrone did something less than fatherly, I wondered if my father were still alive and knew what was going on, would he be OK with how I was being treated.

Coming to terms with all these issues was no easy task, particularly as a child. My default expression was a smile, but when I was alone, my face would stretch as long as a fat bitches realizing someone had eaten the last Twinkie.

I despised the person I had become. My parents didn't realize I was suffering; however, my classmates and teachers saw right through that smile. I was starting to feel like a Lauren Hill song. "Life was strumming my pain with its fingers and killing me softly." While I used to enjoy going to school, it seemed like all I did was have problems. Fighting and yelling at the teachers became a method for venting my rage.

I soaked up negativity like a sponge, turning it into a mischievous DNA infiltrator that tiptoed into my bones and played a game of hide-and-seek in my veins, all without a clue. Technically, the communication dynamics within my family could have been more conducive to open, heartfelt conversations. Instead, there was a tendency to engage in confrontations, left and right hooks, and exchange hurtful remarks.

That girl, whoever I believed I was, had vanished.

Chapter 3

A Twist of Darkness

The school week zoomed by, and all I could think about were the unsolved mysteries within my new life! I couldn't help but fixate on the clock, eagerly anticipating the sound of the bell!

As soon as the bell chimed, the teacher exclaimed, "Please remain seated; our spelling assignments will have a unique twist this week. Each of you will receive a word that may have various meanings and spellings, but they all sound alike. It is up to you to find out the spelling and definition." She stopped speaking long enough to hand out assignments, I was given the word prey, and class ended with a friendly, "Have a great weekend!"

The next week, we all had to present our findings. When it was my turn, I boldly said prey refers to something hunted down and killed by another person, usually for nourishment.

The teacher asked, "Did you find another meaning?"

I said, "Yes, ma'am. Pray is a form of communication with God, where we can converse and be open to his response."

She requested further clarification on the previous statement. Initially, I hesitated for fear of making a mistake. However, the teacher assured me there was no definitive correct or incorrect response. She wanted to understand my thought process. I said, "When I pray, it's important for me to feel like God isn't just hearing my words but also really listening to me. I need to trust that He hears my prayers and answers them in His own special way."

The teacher said, "That's very good!"

I started to understand the importance of *prey* on a deeper level. I was beginning to realize that I, too, was being groomed to gratify a disgusting sexual craving that would ultimately destroy my soul. The word "beautiful" took on an entirely new connotation. Every sick-dick, child-humper with ill intentions first said, "You are so beautiful." Hearing those words made me uncomfortable because I knew a rule was about to be broken; a violation was near.

It felt like all my parents did was stay into it; my stepfather argued, "I saw you all up in this niggah face he was feeling on your ass and shit,
and you didn't even try to stop him; you're a slut."

She would reply, "You bitch ass niggah, you had hickeys on your neck," insult after insult, and it went on for hours. By then, they were both ready to go their separate ways, but as we all know, no one wants to be the first to say their goodbyes.

We began visiting Grandma and Grandpa's place more frequently. I always found it more enjoyable to visit my grandmother, Wilma, but for some reason, circumstances never allowed me to see her.

My mother constantly made excuses like "it's too far" or "there are too many kids." I had a theory; we were being forced into silence. Despite her default statement being "I don't want people in my business," she was always game to take us to my stepfather's side of the family.

Grandma Julie was quite the golfer, always ready to take on the competition in tournaments. She would happily load us up and take us along for the ride. Papa Richard would get us snacks from the concession stand, make sure we were straight, and he would cheer her on. When he gazed at her, he always appeared to be ecstatic. I'm sure once in the boom boom room, he ripped that pussy to shreds!

Golf was supposed to be a silent sport. It was anything but with Papa Richard; when she swayed the club back, he would frequently say, "That's the one right there, that's the one." People would stare, but no one dared to say one word. However, I am sure someone wanted to say, "Hey, shut yo' big black burley-looking ass up!" She would playfully wink and gaze at him; it seemed lighthearted and effortless, embodying the essence of love.

Following the tournament, we would head back home, where she often whipped up a delicious dessert, gave us a refreshing bath, and watched a movie together. I used to spend a lot of time sitting on Papa Richard's lap. It was a different experience from sitting on Papa Jack's lap; there were no uncomfortable coins in his pocket.

Papa Richard had an authoritative demeanor, a rich complexion, and an air of tranquility. I only saw him become upset once, but it was enough to tell me he was about that life!

One afternoon, he took me to the grocery store and let me choose whatever I wanted. I hurriedly set a candy bar on the counter and promptly tucked my hands into my pockets to protect them from the frigid temps.

"Bitch, empty your pockets," the store clerk yelled as he walked down the aisle, having just finished restocking. He must have assumed I was shopping alone, perhaps using food stamps or presenting a note to purchase cigarettes. Who talks to a kid like that? I ignored him because I knew he wasn't talking to me, but when he grabbed my arm, shit got real!

I screamed, "Ouch! Let me go," tears streaming down my cheeks; his hold was as tight as a newborn baby's ass. Papa Richard suddenly appeared from around the corner. His voice was filled with anger as he demanded to know what was happening. He swiftly took hold of the clerk's neck and placed him in a chokehold as if straight out of an action-packed scene from GI Joe.

With a stern expression, he warned, "If you ever put your hands on my granddaughter again, I will kill you!"

The clerk said, "Oh, she's quite an expert at acquiring things; she is a thief. I watched her slipping items into her pocket." Papa Richard stared into my eyes and instructed me to empty my pockets. Knowing that I hadn't taken anything, I did what he asked.

"Well, I don't know what she did with it," the man remarked, "but she had a candy bar."

Papa inquired as to what I had done with the candy bar; I said,

"I put it on the counter; it's where you told me to put it."

The clerk made no apologies. The man yelled, "Get the fuck out of my store, get the fuck out of my store," which we did, but only after my grandfather smacked the shit out of him, daring him to call the cops. Papa Richard was the first ever to defend me; I was getting my ass kicked for far less at home, and no one said anything.

We alternated between spending weekends at my Grandma Julie's and Papa Jack's houses. Papa Jack had a decrepit old house full of stuff that seemed like he might have gotten from Sanford and Son's junkyard as if Lamont himself delivered the shit.

His wife Helen had a captivating appearance, with a petite frame and beautiful, long hair. She was a good cook with a humble personality who loved to sew. She was adamant about keeping me close to her at all times.

We'd arrive on Friday, and she'd faithfully wake us up at nine o'clock in the morning every Saturday for a delicious country-style breakfast. Before we gathered around the table, she would help us dress for the day. While we enjoyed our breakfast, she would prepare herself for an afternoon of shopping. Because Papa Jack made me uncomfortable, I always wanted to accompany her, and I could join her if I finished my breakfast before she got ready.

Papa Jack had an itch that needed scratching; as time passed, he recognized the game and heaped my plate so high that I couldn't eat it. As a result, I couldn't go to the store. Jack had a lengthy history of addiction; he appeared to get out of bed to gargle and swallow vodka; in other words, he was a fucken drunk, and I was stuck with the consequences. An alcoholic looks for a drink in the same way that a pedophile hunts for young pussy, and Papa Jack was no stranger to either habit.

This wasn't his first relapse, and I wasn't his first victim. It was strange the first few times. "You're so beautiful. Kiss me," a soft murmur escaped his lips as he ushered me inside his bedroom. I was so confused I tried to kiss him on the cheek, but instead, he kissed me on the lips.

I still vividly recall his disheveled beard and the putrid smell of alcohol seeping out of his pores. "You like that?" he asked as I backed away.

"No, and I want to go home." We could hear the bouncy station wagon approaching. Papa Jack peered out from behind the curtain. Miss Helen had returned from shopping, so he hastily escorted me out of the room.

Miss Helen asked if I could help her put the groceries away, but she quickly sensed something was wrong and asked if I was OK. I replied, "Yeah, I just wanted to go home." We tried calling home, but they did not answer, leaving me stuck in the trenches with Scruff Mc Gruff!

Each episode of the series became more repulsive than the one before. At first, he would instruct me to say certain things while engaging in self-pleasure. As time passed, the role play grew increasingly intense. He continued to make disgusting comments, "You going to give me some of that pussy." *I was thinking, what pussy? I don't see any cats in here.* I was still confused about his intentions, but it didn't take long for me to figure it out.

During one unexpected encounter, he swiftly approached me, forcefully threw me onto the bed, yanked my pants down, and performed oral sex. I was sobbing and pleading, "Please, this is disgusting.
I'm going to tell my mother."

He aggressively grabbed my neck and violently warned, "If you dare breathe a word, I'll kill your Mama, your sister, and your brother."

Considering the inclination to extend empathy towards individuals dealing with difficulties, it can be quite challenging to differentiate between a genuine plea for assistance. Many individuals struggling with alcoholism often use the sympathy card. Papa Jack always had a never-ending supply of excuses. He always made sure to apologize afterward. I have a drinking problem; I mistook you for

Helen or some strange explanation he thought would justify his behavior as if I should forgive him just because he had an excuse.

Even at an early age, I grasped concepts beyond what others acknowledged. I wasn't convinced by any of that apologetic bullshit. Alcoholism is a pleasurable addiction. Hell, anyone would rather drink than feel thirsty. Jack relished the sensation of power that came from fucking and sucking on children, and he always did it with a sick grin on his face.

Miss Helen's suspicions continued to grow. She frequently questioned me, but I was petrified, so I decided to put on a brave face. She could sense that something was wrong, but I was determined to protect my family from any harm, so I shut what they called the fuck up, put on a smile, and simply expressed my longing for my friends and the comfort of home.

Chapter 4

A New Era of Ambition Emerges

Parenting is a wild ride, a journey full of surprises and no instruction manual to help you along the way. Embracing the unknown and going with the flow is critical, and unfortunately, my parents didn't quite understand either of those concepts. One of my uncles always said that parents should teach their children one of two things: how to work or hustle, following up with, and my kids will indulge in both.

Well, hell, where do I sign up? This sounds like some shit I can get into.

No one seemed to realize that Jessie and I were utterly failing at both. We were only eight years old, but who says learning at a young age is a foolish notion? The old saying "spare the rod, spoil the child" was so true; this reality drove us to victory. No one was spoiling this child. The absurdity of what we were taught was utterly pointless; we were on a fast track to Loserville in Gasoline Drawls!

We weren't going to wait for things to be handed to us, so Jessie and I took matters into our own hands. At our age, we should have been savoring the joys of childhood. However, my circumstances required me to grow up faster than expected. Finding our way worked out. We were aspiring finessers, meticulously ironing out all the unnecessary bullshit before preparing for liftoff; a legendary tale was about to unfold.

One of the most memorable life lessons my parents ever taught me was that making mistakes was not O the Fuck K. If you made a mistake, as Mystical once wisely said. "Aww, you done fucked up now." Who instills in their children the notion that making mistakes is negative? Aren't you supposed to learn from your mistakes?

If it wasn't the error itself that posed a challenge, maybe it was getting caught. We quickly realized making mistakes wasn't the most innovative idea because mistakes were often reinforced with an ass whipping. The philosophy was easy to embrace.

Despite his sharp wit, Jessie couldn't devise a plan to save his life. On the other hand, I thoroughly examined all potential meanings of any given situation. I had a plan B before plan A even went bankrupt. Jessie tried his hand at several clever money-making endeavors, but unfortunately, each was disappointing. He always came and shared the details of what occurred.

I never cared about what went right. Not to become the lead actress starring negative Nancy - that's not it; you see, I've always been curious about what went wrong. My goal was to identify the source of the issue, tweak it, and see what happened next. I would devise an innovative strategy and test it, and lo and behold, it worked like a charm.

He soon recognized that following my instructions would benefit both of us. However, Jessie, being stubborn and armed with unwavering determination, found he learned best through trial and error. With limited opportunities to enjoy the outdoors, I had plenty of free time to brainstorm creative strategies to escape the ghetto. I remember warning him about how his first con would fail, but he wasn't trying to hear shit I said; every flopping detail was planned.

Jessie thought stealing food stamps from the mailbox would be a good idea. I tried to talk him out of it by telling him about the risks and how likely it was that people would probably be waiting for the mail worker to bring their stamps. I asked Jessie about his master plan and his strategy for carrying it out, and he quick-wittedly remarked, "Once the mail girl places them there, I'll snatch them and make a swift getaway!"

I replied, "So, let me get this straight. You're saying that while the mail carrier is present, you plan on stealing food stamps from the mailbox? Seriously, that's it? Is that the grand plan?" I couldn't help but laugh and said sarcastically, "That's not going to work."

He confidently reassured me that his plan was bulletproof. I said, "It will not work, but for shits and giggles, niggah, go for it." That plan, as I expected, got him nowhere fast.

Yep, you betcha the shit didn't work. During our walk to school, Jessie eagerly shared with me how he narrowly escaped being caught by Ms. Pat. #AdrenalineRush #CloseCall. She was a Big Bitch, so I am sure she dreamed about food stamp day! I laughed so hard I thought I might have to take a few puffs from my inhaler. He yelled, "Stop laughing and help me."

Since I was sure he wouldn't give up, I laid it on him thick. "Your first mistake, you should never piss in your living room. You're well known in these projects. Rest assured, your true identity won't remain concealed for much longer, and those with no qualms about exposing a thief will ensure it.

The second blunder was that you should have watched first. Pay close attention to how mother fuckers move, when they come, and when they go. Robbers are lazy; they are not breaking in just because, nor are they speculating on the possibility of a come-up; instead, they are watching or already know what is available for the taking."

Watching the neighborhood's moves was quite a challenge for us as students. Food stamps were mailed in white envelopes, with each recipient receiving their package on a different day. I managed to persuade him to take a stroll around the neighborhood.

Do the houses in the vicinity have a solid financial foundation? Absolutely not! Even though James and Florida Evens' condition improved, they were still borderline broke. Given the size of the projects and the fuckery the place entails, nobody in their right mind would want to live nearby unless absolutely necessary.

Jessie followed some of the advice but not all of it. Despite his impatience, instead of watching, he sneakily started a conversation with the kids who lived nearby and asked them if they were on food stamps. He had an older sister who was well-versed in the welfare system and informed him when people should expect their stamps.

The scheme was successful. Jessie had been stealing food stamps for months, mastering his craft. Occasionally, he would play hooky and venture a mile and a half to different projects. He was prepared to flee with whatever white package he came across. We divided everything between us. Once, I had approximately thirty-five hundred dollars' worth of food stamps.

My parents' situation was rapidly deteriorating; their squabbles had become a daily occurrence. The circumstances became unbearable one evening, so I sought help from my maternal grandfather. He pimped up on her mid-swing, abruptly confronting her about the consequences of continuing such behavior in our presence. He made it clear that she would face repercussions if he heard anything about it again.

After that, they were courteous enough to send us to the room. *Oh, you're so noble; how kind!* Nevertheless, the gesture proved to be pointless as she continued to show her ass in our presence. Yet, when tensions escalated, Dad would eventually instruct us to go outside. Strangely enough, I found solace in their arguments, as it allowed me to experience a sense of independence.

Independence seemed like a far-fetched fantasy. As their situation deteriorated, the beatings took on a more unconventional nature. For instance, instead of simply grabbing my shirt, Dad gripped my entire titty with the sweater. On another occasion, he kicked me right in the crack of my dookie shoot.

This Nigga forcefully propelled me across the room as if he were preparing to kick a field goal. As a result, I required seven stitches. DHS would have devoured their monkey ass, so I had to pretend that I had fallen. I'll never comprehend how they managed to escape without consequences, considering the Adidas Sign was still lodged in the crack of my ass!

It was a typical Friday, with mom and dad arguing and screaming. During this battle, a never-ending downward spiral began. My mom discovered that Tyrone was involved in a romantic entanglement with a woman employed at the courthouse.

Tyrone seemed to prefer women of greater stature, which prompted Mom to seek employment. He wasn't being productive either, so it was hypocritical of the Pot to criticize the Kettle.

After countless job search struggles, my mother finally landed a third-shift position. She was working two or three nights a week at a job that was supposed to be full-time, but many of the cargo didn't arrive when they were supposed to. The work was slow, and the workers were faster than expected.

Our dad kindly offered to watch us while mom worked in the evenings. The fact that she worked the third shift meant he would have more time to fuck off with the ladies. So long as it served its intended purpose, who am I to pass judgment?

I awoke one night to the sound of the vacuum sweeper. They were both neat freaks. I assumed Mom had arrived home early from work and was cleaning, but that was not the case.

Tyrone was standing in the middle of the floor, naked, with his dick caught in the vacuum hose. I hurried to the bathroom and jumped back into bed, expecting to forget about it, but the vision was still there, buried in my subconscious; that image would never leave.

The distinct echo of footsteps resonated through the silence, followed by the slow, ominous creak of the door swinging open. "Did you see that?" he asked with a hint of curiosity as he entered the room. "Don't let your mother in on our secret," he quipped. After I agreed, his unsettling follow-up question came, "Did you like what you saw?" I answered, "No, I'm not sure what I saw." He exposed his private area and lightly grazed it against my arm. I winced and hid my arm beneath the covers. Upon catching a glimpse of my face, he hastily exited the room. The rest of the night was spent tossing and turning. That was the last time Tyrone did anything of that nature, yet that wouldn't be the last time the topic was raised.

I told my mother about Tyrone's actions the next day, and they argued. I couldn't have cared less; I wanted to escape that place, so I quickly got my siblings ready and headed to school. Although I was eager to tell Jessie the news, I buried it with the rest of my soul's misery because it was too embarrassing to bring up when I got in his face.

My mom advised us to go outside and play after we arrived home. We were only allowed to play outside when they were broken up or she had a dick appointment. *Aww, Mommy dearest, you mean we can go outside? Today has to be our lucky day! Come on down; you are the next contestant on the Outside is Right!* She pretended to be doing us a favor, lady, please, you are having company. I know the drill.

"Where is Dad?" Kyle enquired.

Mom answered, "I kicked your dad out! I am sick of him." Imagine that he nearly got me to wear a dick bracelet, but she got *tired* of him and dethroned him. That, without a doubt, left a shit stain on my heart.

After spending so much time outside, we decided to take the initiative and go inside. The streetlights had officially turned on, giving the project an eerie, abandoned atmosphere. Even though we could still hear her in the room making her ooh daddy noises, we let her fuck in peace.

My mom would lock all the windows and doors when they were fighting.

The phone rang, and my brother answered and replied, "I'm not sure, Daddy. Yes, she is in the room. Okay, bye."

After about ten minutes, Tyrone began pounding on the door, "Let me in. Got Dammit, let me in."

"Mom, Dad is here," I said as I knocked on the bedroom door.

"Just don't let him in," she adamantly stated. After her remark, a deafening noise reached my ears. I hurriedly went to see what was happening. I watched as Dad skillfully shattered the window, reminiscent of a scene out of MacGyver or an action movie; perhaps his previous combat training had equipped him for this moment.

Whatever it was, he leaped through the glass with a daring acrobatic roll, his body gracefully twisting and turning in mid-air. He landed on his feet, rushed into her room, and got to snap, crackle, and popping on her ass

We hurried into our rooms, absolutely terrified. While they were WWFing in the kitchen, her boy toy hurriedly escaped, making it clear that he wasn't going to jeopardize his life for the sake of pussy. I guess he was thinking on the way out, "I murdered the cat, not getting murdered over it!"

Resuming their usual Broadway-worthy theatrics, my mother and Tyrone turned our humble living room into a stage for their verbal gladiator match. The air crackled with the electricity of their ceaseless exchange of insults, each one more creative than the last. It was like watching a tennis match if the players were hurling insults instead of balls! The only love consistent in this house was the love of drama!

This verbal jousting lasted two hours and was akin to a relentless emotional roller coaster without the safety bar and the overpriced popcorn. It was a marathon of wit and will, a test of who could come up with the most inventive insult. Who does this? I could not wrap my head around any of this.

Tyrone finally exited, but his parting words were neither witty nor memorable. They were remarkably mundane. "I'm off to fetch some milk," he declared. And with that simple statement, the metaphorical curtain fell, marking his departure from the house.

The next morning felt like any other day. We got ready for school, cleaned up, and went off to embrace the day. As soon as I stepped out the front door, I was greeted by the sight of my father dangling from a tree.

I shouted for my mother, and my siblings burst into tears, unable to be comforted. When the paramedics arrived, Dad was quickly taken to the hospital, where he stayed for approximately a week. They both seemed to be quite desperate for attention, manipulating any situation for a reconciled finale; Yes, they got their ignorant asses back together.

Tonae and Bianca came over to check on me the day after my dad's attempted suicide. We talked for hours through the window, deciding to devise a strategy to get me out of the house or, at the very least, give us some extra time after school. Hell, I would have gone to bible studies to get out of the house. After hours of brainstorming, we came up with the 4-H club or the crossing guards because I had recently reached the minimum age required to join.

I've always been quite the talker, so the following day, I headed to school and spun them a clever story about my desire to be more responsible, convincing them that I would be a perfect match as a crossing guard. Mission Accomplished. The school hired me as a crossing guard. Tonae asked the 4-H leader to converse with my mother, who graciously agreed to let me become a member if my mom agreed. Surprisingly enough, she said yes.

Even though there was no monetary compensation, I was okay with it. Freedom! Now, I knew firsthand what Phil Collins meant. "I have been waiting for this moment all my life." Now that it was mine, I'd do anything to keep it. I made it a point to excel in 4-H; I always received excellent Clover awards. I got compliments on my crossing guard duties and improved my classroom demeanor; I was also less angry. Or was it the quiet before the storm?

As I previously stated, I would have attended a bible study to keep myself out of inevitable jams, and that is precisely what I did. I had bible studies on Saturdays. I told the teacher I could only come every other Saturday. Miss Betty agreed that any church was better than none, so I scheduled the Saturdays to correspond with the weekends I was supposed to be at Papa Jack's.

Bible studies wasn't too bad. As my interest in Miss Betty's lessons grew. I pleaded with her for permission to be baptized. She posed several inquiries regarding Jesus, the significance of baptism, and my comprehension of its meaning.

I must have aced the test because the following day, she reached out to my parents on my behalf to request their permission. My father became outraged, labeled her a "Bitch," and launched into an angry tirade about the white man's plan to abolish or distort religion in black communities. In other words, he snapped, and the excellent adventures of Jesus Christ ended.

Jessie and I had extra time to hang out now that I had more freedom. After patrol duties, Jessie would frequently wait for me and accompany me home. As with anything, after a while, certain things get old.

Jessie was itching with anticipation, eager to dive headfirst into another daring venture. "I'm in dire need of some money," he confessed, his voice laced with a desperate edge. "I mean, there's only so much one can do with stolen food stamps. The thrill of swiping candy has lost its

charm: I need something more. I need cold, hard cash."

"Well, my mother occasionally makes us break down food stamps for gas money," I explained. "You could ask your sister if she knows someone looking to buy food stamps."

The following day, he returned to school with two hundred dollars in his pocket. He eagerly shared his story with a playful tone, mentioning how his sister had connected him with a buyer. I couldn't help but ask, "Did you give them a bunch of stamps?"

"I gave them six hundred," he cleverly replied. I informed him that it was meant to be divided in half, and his sister graciously accepted her portion as a finder's fee. You do better when you know better; she never caught him slipping again.

He generously shared a portion of each sale with her, totaling around fifty bucks. Ultimately, he had accumulated approximately fifteen hundred and graciously gave me five.

Although Jessie wasn't thrilled with the food stamps scheme, it was clear that the hustle had evolved into something more than just a profit-driven venture. It had also acquired a potential element of danger. Given that everyone had caught on and was actively searching for the Food Stamp Caper, it was only a matter of time before calamity struck.

The seasons were shifting. I loved fresh fruits and vegetables. A farmer nearby grew about three acres of every crop imaginable. Jessie would slash through the field to reduce the possibility of people noticing him on city streets. He used to bring me fresh fruit as a surprise. The plums and nectarines were the most delicious I'd ever tasted. Then it dawned on me: if they could profit from their crops, so could we!

My thoughts immediately went to devising a plan to steal the vegetables without being caught. I came up with some ideas but needed something more solid. We grew up in a hick town; there were always farmers' market stands around us. Even though we were in the city's lower reaches, walking up a hill opened a new world of lovely homes with manicured lawns and no stray beer bottles. *Excuse me while I raise my church finger; there's money to be made, and it's time to get it!*

I casually inquired if Jessie still had his trusty old wagon. He confirmed its existence with a nod and a single word, "Yes."

"Why don't we pay our hardworking farmers a visit?" I suggested with a mischievous glint in my eye. "We could fill that wagon of yours with tomatoes, snap peas, green beans, you name it. Then, we could turn into impromptu salesmen, trek up the hill, and try our luck selling
the fruits of someone else's labor. What do you say, partner?"

Jessie had a sharp sense of humor; he was a quick-witted asshole. "Transporting something uphill, especially since your black ass is restricted to the front yard, can be quite a challenge," he said with a playful chuckle. He was right, so I chose to refrain from voicing my less-than-positive comments.

Considering the importance of flawlessness, it was essential for the plan to be foolproof. Be prepared for some serious repercussions if any errors are made. This plan had some flaws, but it also had some positive aspects that gave it confidence. Nothing beats a failure but a try.

As I focused on the rest of the plan, I encouraged Jessie to try it. The following Saturday, he cleverly maneuvered past the gate separating the farmer from the projects. With a quick and clever mind, he gathered all he could carry in his backpack and set off on his journey up the hill, earning around fifty dollars.

Chapter 5

Whispers Within Secluded Spaces

Even at the tender age of nine, I quickly realized that I had no intention of putting up with any bullshit from anyone. My life was like a soap opera that had overdosed on caffeine: relentless, dramatic, and seemingly allergic to commercial breaks. Just when I thought the director had finally yelled 'cut,' life would deliver another plot twist my way, ensuring the ratings stayed high and the popcorn kept popping.

As a result of the incident involving the vacuum sweeper, my mother was forced to change her shift and hire a babysitter. We began going to Millie's, a fat, funky mother fucker who appeared to fall asleep while eating peanut butter and jelly sandwiches.

I hated going over there. I've never been a fan of scents, and the smell at Millie's was nothing short of dreadful. Millie was a marijuana smoker and quite the social butterfly. Her home was always buzzing with a constant stream of visitors.

When our mother brought us inside, Millie would playfully act as if she fucked with us. "Hey, my babies, how are y'all doing?" She would cleverly wait for my mother to disappear from view before instructing us to enter the room, which only contained a pissed-out mattress and two soc um bop um toys.

We could not leave the room for any portion of the day and went without food all day! I had cultivated a more introverted nature. Recently, I'd noticed a peculiar shyness sprouting within me, a sort of self-imposed gag order that had been keeping my thoughts on a tight leash. It seemed that every time I mustered up the audacity to let my ideas loose, more often than not, it ended with me sporting a bloody lip, a souvenir from the battlefield of conversation. Nobody seemed to notice that my spirit had become impregnated with rage, and shit was getting ready to hit the fan.

Millie took care of us for approximately a month. My mother's top priority was ensuring we never went hungry, so she diligently prepared our lunches daily. Unfortunately, we never had the chance to enjoy a meal.

Millie followed a consistent daily routine: inspect the bag, store the food in the refrigerator, and then send us back to the room. Whenever we needed to use the bathroom, we had to resort to banging on the door to get her attention. On top of that, she only allowed us to have one cup of juice per day.

Our last day under Millie's care was wild. Candice mentioned that she was hungry. I knocked on the door, and after receiving no response, I decided to leave the room. I informed Ms. Millie that Candace was

hungry. Millie responded, "Get your ass back in that room."

"My mother..." I exclaimed.

Ms. Millie rudely interrupted me before I could finish my sentence! Delivering a mighty punch to my back as if she were channeling her inner Donkey Kong. She hollered, "Didn't I tell you to get your ass in that room?"

I stared at her for about three seconds to ensure that the impulse would not turn into regret. Nope, this was happening, and there was no turning back. I pounced on her ass like a spider monkey. Who in their right mind would dare lay a hand on someone's child without any valid reason? Not to mention that she was a childcare provider. Can't you lose your license for shit like that? Yeah, nothing about Millie screamed professional, so I am sure the thought never crossed her mind.

Millie contacted my mother and informed her that I had gone insane and attacked her and that she should pick us up and find a new babysitter. That was music to my ears! When my mom arrived, she didn't bother asking any questions. Instead, she placed all the blame on me.

I had to put up with her continued grumbling about how I was making things tough for her on the trip home. I couldn't care less about her comments, which entered one ear and immediately exited the other. I was fully aware of the typical phrase that awaited me: "I'm fucking you up when we get home."

Candace and Kyle were confused; they had no idea what had occurred because they had come out of the room at the ass end, barely catching a glimpse of the chaotic scene. My mother grilled poor Candace like she was a suspect in a high-stakes crime, all because she was determined to catch me in a little white lie. "Candace said we were hungry, and the fat lady ate our food." Kyle chimed in, "She punched her in the back when Sister told her to give us our food."

My Mom shot Kyle a menacing look and said, "Kyle, you couldn't help but throw in your two cents?"

Despite the stories matching perfectly, she couldn't resist pointing the finger at me. According to her, I had a unique talent. I was only good at one thing: fucking up. Who knew I had such an exceptional talent? *Lady, fuck you, come beat my ass so I can get some sleep!*

As promised, I got my ass kicked after we got home. Mom then called around, talking about me like a dog to anyone listening. But bizarre as it may seem, I didn't care about that whipping; it felt good to defend myself, and there was plenty more to come.

There was a woman named Francine who lived next door to us. Every day, she'd look out the window and ask about my day. Francine was always thoughtful, consistently surprising me with various fruits like apples and oranges.

It was a mystery how she always managed to know what I liked. I never engaged in a conversation with her; I never disclosed my preferences. Francine would hand me a few dollars every Friday morning and cheerfully say, "Treat yourself to something for Fun Friday!"

I used to chuckle, pondering the usefulness of a mere two dollars. I had that young moolah baby, cash, perhaps more than any of the adults in my life had put together. Without even batting an eye, I split the cash that Francine slipped me, tossing a buck to my sister and another to my brother.

I didn't make any purchases on Friday. Instead, I thought it would be a good idea to tighten my purse straps and stash the cash. I was still trying to wrap my head around it, but I had a feeling that I'd have everything I needed when the time came. I'd soon uncover the true motive behind Francine's sudden kindness towards me.

My mother decided to enroll in beauty school. After I damn near smacked the previous babysitter into a coma, I realized it was essential to take charge and control the narrative. It was the least I could do. I asked Mom about the possibility of Francine staying with us.

I couldn't help but mention how ridiculously close it was to our house, and I volunteered to handle the bedtime preparations so she wouldn't have to lift a finger when she got home. She was all in, no questions asked. I introduced her to Ms. Francine. Francine graciously offered to watch us for free.

Francine was an enjoyable babysitter. We had a great time playing games together, and she even trusted me enough to let me braid her hair. Having a trustworthy person to confide in and share my innermost thoughts with was extremely helpful. I thought I had finally found someone who truly understood my perspective and with whom I could be sincere. She looked after us for three months, and everything was going well. However, things are only sometimes as they seem!

One day, I walked through the door after a long day of school, only to find my mother waiting for me. Usually, she wouldn't be home until eight o'clock. I asked what she was doing at home, and she murmured something about not having school today. Oh, I shrugged my shoulders and asked, "So, can we go outside?"

We'd gotten into the habit of arriving home and Francine letting us play outside as long as we pledged to keep it a secret. "No," my mother said, "but you can tell Francine I said come here." I did just as she requested.

Francine arrived promptly, without any hesitation. When we walked in, my mother wasted no time putting her paws to Francine's drawls; she was hitting Francine anywhere she could.

"Mom, what's going on? What in the world are you doing? That's enough. You really need to stop!" I exclaimed; my voice trembled with fear. I couldn't resist trying to break it up; it was so heartbreaking to watch, so I grabbed my mother's arm and screamed, "Mom, stop, get off of her." But my mom, with her superhuman strength, effortlessly pushed me across the room like a ragdoll. She continued beating on
Francine's ass until she was tired.

I was so confused. I felt terrible because I marched Francine straight into an ambush. I wondered if she thought I had set her up. Her eyes were enormous, resembling those of a colossal squid, and the dark circles beneath them had transformed into bruises.

I had never witnessed such a brutal beating before. Francine attempted to fight back, but the more she fought, the worse it got. She ended up curled up on the couch like Ace Ventura.

My mom apparently decided it was a good time for a Kit Kat bar and took a break. Maybe she was hungry. The Snicker commercial makes it plain: you're just not yourself when you're hungry. Well, I guess Mom must have been absolutely famished with the way she was acting! While on her pound time intermission, she called Tyrone, who was cutting the yard for Grandma Julie.

She told him to come to the house immediately, all while carefully assuring him that everything was perfectly fine. Although buried within the depths of my soul, I had a feeling that things were definitely not alright. I couldn't help but think that the universe was determined to take a detour into bullshit land before finding its way back to normalcy!

Francine was sitting on the couch; my mother warned her that she better not leave the fucken house. I tried to smuggle her some water as I inquired about her well-being. She was so terrified that she pissed on the sofa. You'd think it was World War Three up in there. My mother beat her ass again, forcing her to wash the couch covers and sit on the floor in the corner until Tyrone came; this was the most degrading shit I had ever seen. *Who gives a grown woman a time-out?*

Tyrone walked in and saw Francine in the corner; he already knew what time it was. Mom did not discriminate; she tore his ass up too. I
was so confused. I said, "Francine, just run, get out of here."

My Mom was on Tyrone like white on rice. Mom began beating him with a nightstick. I had no idea where she got it from, but you could see the life leaving his body; Dad was pleading with us to run to the payphone and call the cops.

My mother instructed my little sister to get a knife; I think she had lost her whole damn mind. Why would you think it would be ok for you to tell someone to get a knife to kill their father? While our dear old dad was on his knees, practically begging us to dial the boys in blue, we stood there, as still as statues, in total disbelief.

We did not need to lift a finger, let alone a phone. In an attempt to save what was left of her secret lover's ass, Francine dialed those three well-known digits, 911, quicker than the flurry of blows my mom delivered upside her head. Ain't no way in hell I would have been worried about him. My initial instinct would have been self-preservation: *The ship is going down, bitch save yourself!*

As the sound of sirens in the distance grew louder, we returned to our rooms. Kyle and Candice were devastated; their cries echoed throughout the house. The police showing up was quite a scene. Francine stepped forward, ready to present her piece, stating she had heard screams and babysits us and just wanted to make sure we were all okay. One of the officers, taken aback by the sight of her eye, inquired, "Holy shit, what happened to your eye?"

Francine glanced at my mother and yelled, "A big black mosquito bit me!"

Out of nowhere, I got this wild itch to start buzzing like a damn mosquito, all while pointing at my mom. However, I knew I would have been anything but safe. Mom would have ripped me a new asshole on the spot. It felt like a scene from a crime drama without the piss poor detective and intense background music. Despite the disturbing scene, no arrests were made. The police officers patiently waited for my dad to finish packing before taking off. I had a feeling that as soon as he walked out the door, my safety would be anything but guaranteed. Even though I managed to avoid a beating, she couldn't help but lecture me about my lack of loyalty, my boldness in telling Francine to flee, and my questionable choice to defend the enemy.

I was so surprised I didn't get my ass handed to me. Perhaps it was because she had beaten so many asses that she didn't have the energy nor stamina for one more, but it was most likely that she had a scheduled dick rendezvous planned.

She instructed us to eat, shower, and go to bed. It took me a minute to unwind. As I was about to doze off, a sudden knock on the door interrupted our tranquility. Without hesitation, Mom swiftly made her way to our bedroom door and closed it. Just as I suspected, my suspicions were spot on! A Dick appointment was definitely the case! I glanced out the window, and what do you know, there was that familiar car once more!

Mom had a couple of regulars who came and dropped it off in her drawls consistently; one of them was very cool. I attended school with his daughter and saw him picking her up after school, but I refrained from commenting as I was aware of the dynamics involved. Several of my friends' parents were engaging in questionable behavior, so I was familiar with the unspoken game rules.

I liked his daughter, and we got along well. Apparently, her mother found out what her boyfriend and my mom were up to and sent her on a bogus mission, and she paid the price. "Your mother is a whore," she commented one day as I put up my flag after patrol.

I did not agree, but I didn't disagree either, but because everyone was present, I said, "Your momma and Petunia Pig are twins: fat bitches," she kicked me.

As the teacher turned the corner, she was greeted by the unexpected sight of me forcefully extending my foot toward her chest. She escorted me to the office, where I received a stern talking to, and unfortunately, lost my position as a crossing guard. I was livid. All I could think about was being trapped in the house with no escape route.

Tonae, Bianca, and Jessie were patiently waiting for me. I was crying uncontrollably when I shared with them what had occurred. Everyone assumed I was crying because I would get in trouble, but that didn't faze me; ass whippings had become a breakfast for champions. The problem was that I was on the verge of losing the small amount of freedom I had grown to cherish.

Right as we're about to make it back home, I hear the unmistakable sound of screeching tires and doors flinging open. As I spun around, I couldn't help but notice the girl and her mother. The girl quickly jumped out, but her mother, on the other hand, was desperately trying to break free. Her belly was lodged in the steering wheel.

I shouted, "Maybe if we grease that pig up, she'll be able to wiggle her way out of this situation!" The onlookers couldn't help but burst into laughter. With a squelch that could shatter glass, the woman rolled out of the car, breaking free from the clutches of the steering wheel piercing her side.

She shrieked at her daughter, "You better beat her ass right now!" Possibly presuming her daughter didn't hear her, she continued, "I mean it. You better beat her ass right fucking now!"

I gave her a fair warning that if she had the audacity to lay a finger on me, she better be ready for history's echo; because she was getting fucked up again, not to mention that I had lost my job! *Girl, walk away; honey, walk away!*

Maybe feeling more scared of her mother than of me, she smacked the hell out of me, and I returned the favor in a polite but firm manner. I tore her ass up. I guess her mom didn't appreciate the fact that her daughter was slapped around like a two-dollar whore, so she jumped in and started hitting me.

I grabbed a shattered bottle, jugging it into the woman's arm. Someone from the crowd ran and told my mom what was happening.

My mom raced around that corner with the speed of Lightning McQueen, sporting a one-of-a-kind bra and pants combination that undoubtedly turned a few heads. Mom went in on that woman and proceeded to beat the living daylights out of her. And the fun didn't end there. I began digging in her eye as if I had stumbled upon a pot of gold, nearly dislodging her eyeball from her skull. I'm not sure her children had ever witnessed anything like this; her daughter pleaded with us to leave her mom alone.

After the police showed up and put an end to the chaos, Petunia's twin was whisked away in an ambulance. The next time I laid eyes on her, she was rocking a fashionable eye patch. These two consecutive encounters brought out a fierce side of me that I never knew existed, and nobody was prepared for the fight that was about to ensue.

The Fourth of July was approaching, and I always looked forward to visiting my mother's parents' house for the holiday. Their parties were always off the charts. Everyone possessed a remarkable talent for culinary expertise and the art of barbecuing. The sides and dessert were incredibly impressive. The entire spread was fire! And it's worth mentioning there was never a dull moment.

I'd hang out with my cousins while the grown folks cracked jokes and had a good time playing cards. With my aunts and mother also being fans of dancing, I knew we were in for a great time as long as the music kept playing. If the music stopped, it signified shit had hit the fan, or the party was over. Just thinking about the excitement filled me with joy for the remainder of the week.

At long last, the highly anticipated Fourth of July made its grand entrance. We were dressed in red, white, and blue as if our shit didn't stink, even though we were probably the funkiest mother fuckers in the place with the chaos we had going on. We were unquestionably patriotic, dysfunctional, but patriotic, nonetheless. My father would accompany us, but my mother acted brand new in front of her sisters, so you could guarantee they'd fight when we got home.

That year, we skipped visiting my grandma's. Someone in town threw an epic Fourth of July bash complete with delicious food, breathtaking fireworks, and loads of fun for the whole family. My mother and her sisters even decided to get in on the action by participating in a dancing competition. I knew there would be a severe problem as soon as the Dog Catcher started playing!

They were on their way, one by one, each showcasing their unique canine-inspired moves. Their performances were undoubtedly entertaining, from the freaky dog to the nasty dog. Hell, one was out there panting like a poodle. As the crowd gathered around them, the men were passionately cheering and shouting like a group of broke dick dogs.

Tyrone was seething with anger; his face turned red with fury. He had a mischievous plan to sabotage the dance contest because he wasn't a fan of my mother's dance moves. As a result, he continuously dispatched my sister and me to go on the dance floor and ask her questions, but she skillfully brushed us off. Every time we returned; he would promptly send us out again.

My mother was so furious that she eventually dropped out of the contest. We were constantly manipulated, mere pieces in their elaborate power struggle, as if it were normal. After that fight, Tyrone claimed he was moving in with his mother.

Because I wasn't on patrol anymore, I was back at the window, calling shots. Jessie was on my ass about the Farmer and the Dell plan. I knew the Farmer grew a wide range of crops. I researched and discovered that the most popular and profitable vegetables were sweet corn, green tomatoes, and snap beans.

As I explained the concept and what we would do, Jessie became excited. His eyes twinkled with the potential of cash. When it came to money, Jessie was like a junkie chasing their first high.

Every Thursday night, my mother would set off on her exciting escapades. Despite residing in different homes, she and Tyrone found a way to sustain their relationship. Jessie always gathered the crops after school on Thursdays. With a clever touch, Jessie would quietly deliver the produce to the back door, perfectly synchronized with my parents' departure. I eagerly anticipated the drop.

My parents' behavior was full of surprises, so the night could have been brief or lengthy. When they went out, a couple of interesting things could occur when they returned: an intense sexcapade or heated arguments. I recognized the significance of acting fast if I wanted to have a chance of achieving my goals. I thoroughly washed the vegetables before placing them at the back door.

After school on Friday, it was our routine to visit my grandparents' place. Jessie never missed a beat, selling the crops every Saturday like clockwork. We consistently increased our earnings week after week, reaching at least two hundred dollars per week. And without fail, he would generously give me half of it on Mondays or bring it to me after finishing his work on the weekends that we stayed with Grandma Julie.

I never particularly enjoyed the second and fourth weekend of the month. My siblings and I spent those weekends at Papa Jack's; as luck would have it, this was his weekend. Upon our arrival, Papa Jack was on high alert, but I had a sneaky plan up my sleeve. As I pondered, I couldn't help but chant, "Your eyes might shine, your teeth might grit, but this little Pussy you will not get!" *Not this weekend, no, Sir.*

I was itching to hit the stores and stock up on bags and supplies for the crops. Imagine if we jazzed up the bags with artistic flair; buyers would practically throw their money at us! After breakfast was ready, I quickly finished and eagerly waited at the door for Ms. Helen.

Jack was fuming with anger. I was worried his ass was going to burst into flames. Survival was the name of the game, and I was willing to go to great lengths to come out on top. I was overjoyed that I had outwitted the fox and returned home beaming with happiness, but all good things must come to an end. Some things, I suppose, are inevitable.

Chapter 6

The Truth is a Snake's Greatest Adversary

Following the incident with Francine, my mother decided it was best to take a break from school. Three weeks later, Mom revealed that she had chosen to withdraw from school due to her ongoing struggle with finding a babysitter, but she found another job working the first shift. After handing Francine's ass to her for fucking our father, Mom asked if we knew about their shenanigans.

Imagine that; mother fuckers could care less until Dick was involved. It would have been wise for her to ask plenty of questions after the first or second interaction with the weird-ass babysitters. Nope, there was none of that; perhaps it was too much like right!

Now, it made perfect sense. Francine knew so much of what I liked because this Niggah was straight pillow-talking, and she sent us outside so they could fuck. I completely understood why mom swarmed on their ass like flies on shit. Fucking my niggah is one thing, but fucking my niggah in my home is quite another.

If it had been me, I would have dug up her mammie and smacked the dust off her bones for her lack of home training. This incident was one of the few times in my life that I agreed with my mother. I won't lie, the shit was epic. She skated all over her ass as if she were competing in the Winter Olympics for the gold medal.

Mama had an uncanny ability to light up those cancer sticks. Every time we visited the store, "Virginia Slim Menthol" was a phrase that always seemed to come up. On this particular day, she was puffing away on one cigarette after another. Her smoking habit really kicked into high gear during their heated arguments. As the pack vanished into thin air, I couldn't help but notice her growing increasingly agitated, tense, and incredibly angry. She was like a ticking time bomb, ready to explode.

My siblings and I were having a funky good time! Mom screamed at us to locate a chair, sit the fuck down, and shut the fuck up. Why bother with a chair when we're already chilling on the floor? Clearly, she had lost her mind. She couldn't sit still; Her feet seemed to have a mind of their own, constantly tapping away in a rhythmic movement. Well, her behavior was definitely giving off some serious *what the fuck* vibes. It had a certain Eddie Kane Jr. feel to it.

Mom usually drove us to the store, but this time, she asked us to walk and get cigarettes for her. In those days, all the cashier needed was a note stating the child was allowed to purchase cigarettes. I found it odd that she wanted us to walk; we had only done that once before. Based on her behavior, I was OK with it; it was best to give her some space. It was roughly a mile to the store.

While walking, my siblings imitated fight scenes from the archives of Mom and Dad's greatest hits. We marveled at how she choked him and how he threw change at us. Kyle scratched in the mud with a stick,
"Suck my dick!"

Candice jumped dead on his ass, "You ain't got no dick bitch."

He said, "Shut the fuck up."

"Or what?" she answered. Candice stayed ready. She was always up for a fight, which was undoubtedly advantageous. Staying ready eliminates the need to get ready!

I was always conscious of my surroundings, probably because I never knew what would happen next, and I couldn't get comfortable. A man appeared to be watching us from the other side of the street.

I moved to the other side of the road so we could be behind him, but mostly to see what he'd do.

He crossed to the opposite side of the street and continued walking at the same pace as we did. I had a bad feeling something sinister was happening, and I wouldn't say I liked it. Three more blocks passed, with his route remaining unchanged. I centered my attention on him.

I couldn't help but notice the gradual dimming of his eyes, morphing into an abyss of darkness, as if he didn't care about anything or anyone.

I was terrified, but I remembered Miss Betty saying that no weapon formed against me would prosper. When I was scared or didn't know what to do, she told me to plead the blood of Jesus over my life. After I finished praying, his demonic figure materialized before my very eyes. Evilness took control immediately, creating an unsettling atmosphere that sent chills down my spine.

I told my siblings I was worried that the man would hurt us. "I'm just going to shove this stick up his ass," Candace said as she grabbed the stick from Kyle.

"Nobody is shoving sticks up anybody's ass," I responded, grabbing the stick from her. "I'm going one way, and you're going the other. Run home and tell mom I ran towards the store and to come and help me."

Kyle agreed, but my sister was crying and refused to leave me. I advised them to run and run fast. I would be OK; the best thing they could do for me was get help. Unfortunately, that help never arrived.

After I yelled, "RUN," we quickly made our escape. My siblings and I hauled ass in opposite directions. This dude was hot on my trail, like a bloodhound on my scent. He just wouldn't quit!

Completely immersed in his thoughts, he narrowly escaped being hit by a passing automobile, blissfully unconscious of the commotion of angry drivers and wailing horns he left behind. He appeared unconcerned, like who cares if these people could be witnesses to your meticulously orchestrated offense; he had stalked his prey and was determined to have his way, which was all that mattered to him.

I hurriedly approached a porch and began vigorously knocking on the door, like the white girl in the movies who was uncertain about her next move or where to seek refuge. Yet, it was evident that he relished the idea of defying his target as he trapped me on the porch.

I continued banging on the door, yelling, "Help, please stop!" With a sudden burst of aggression, my clothes were violently torn from my body, and a mighty blow struck my face. And just like that, I had another story to add to my portfolio of misery.

Thank God, a woman was home; she came out and began beating him with a shovel like a Hebrew slave. That did not bother him in the least. We fought tooth and nail against him until he was compelled to retreat. My emotions were running high, preventing me from shedding tears.

However, after the dust settled and I had a chance to reflect, I could no longer hold back my tears and let out a loud yell, "Why God?" I couldn't stop wondering why God let these things happen to me despite my best efforts.

I wasn't old enough to be dealing with karma. Why did I have to suffer? Despite this man's violation of me, all I could think about was getting some cigarettes for my mother. I realized it would be an additional hell to pay if I came into the house without them. I graciously thanked the woman for her help and told her I had to leave to pick up cigarettes for my mom.

"Baby, there's no way you'll get any cigarettes like this," the woman said. My clothes were torn, my hair was matted, and the priceless locket that held the picture of me, Tonae, and Bianca had vanished. My mouth and fingernails were both bleeding from fiercely digging and clawing into his skin. The woman had a heart full of compassion and a severe sense of empathy. She handed me a jacket, gave me a warm hug, and assured me everything would be fine; I knew it would be anything but.

I offered to walk home, but she insisted on giving me a ride. What would cause someone to willingly get into a car with a total stranger right after such a devastating attack? Nevertheless, I made the bold choice to take a chance.

She drove me home after going to the store and purchasing cigarettes. As we approached the house, a wave of anxiety washed over me, leaving me feeling unsettled about how the conversation would unfold.

I was grateful to have the woman by my side as I was utterly petrified.

Upon entering the room, I noticed my siblings casually relaxing on the couch while my mother calmly folded towels. I was so relieved they were safe that I didn't worry about myself; my only concern was that they were OK.

The woman began the conversation by saying, "I wanted to inform you that I brought your daughter home because she was sexually assaulted by a man on my porch. I beat him with a shovel. Your daughter was scratching, and I was hitting. I'm confident we both have evidence beneath our nails; I suggest contacting the authorities so that we can give our statements." The woman went on to say, "I will never forget his expression! I drew a mental image of this mother fucker in my head, and he must pay the price."

"I'm going to wait until my boyfriend gets here, and we'll handle it," my mother said calmly.

The woman cleverly countered, aiming to be empathetic yet still challenging my mother's thought process, suggesting that we inform the police immediately to safeguard all evidence. The woman also suggested that my mom pack my clothes in a bag, anticipating they might also want to inspect them.

"Whenever my boyfriend gets off, I will take her; I don't want to deal with this alone," my mother said emphatically. My mother explained that she was in a similar situation and did not want to go through this alone.

The woman placed her palm over her mouth, gasping for air, and said, "Oh my gosh, I'm sorry to hear that. It must be tough to accept that history has repeated itself." The woman kindly shared her contact information, offering her assistance whenever my mom decided to contact the police. She assured us she would provide a statement whenever the time came. Although my mother expressed gratitude for bringing me home, her demeanor was anything but.

I was sick to my stomach; all I wanted to do was take a shower. I wished for things I knew would never happen. I wanted my mother to say, "Come here, baby, you're going to be OK," and walk me through my feelings and emotions. Wishful Fucking thinking!

No, Sir, when that woman left, I got my ass beat; I took too long with the cigarettes, and she's convinced I was out being fast and made the whole thing up. Oh really, please explain these bleeding Bushwick Bill hands. Let me guess: my mind is playing tricks on me. Get the fuck out of here!

The authorities were never notified, justice was never achieved, and if anything, ever left a mark, it was the clear lack of concern she displayed for my well-being. She didn't even attempt to seek medical help. In that moment, it dawned on me just how small and insignificant I truly was, how little importance I held, and how effortlessly others could manipulate me without facing any repercussions.

As I received each lick, my siblings shed silent tears. Even with tears streaming down her face, I could sense a profound discontent simmering in Candice's gaze. Despite my brother's sadness, he recognized that he could only do so much to help. After finishing my shower, I headed straight to bed, where I lay lost in my thoughts, questioning the meaning of it all: *Is this truly what life is?* I began contemplating whether I should commit suicide. I also wondered if other girls were going through similar difficulties.

It was crystal clear and impossible to deny I was caught in a storm of emotions, and no matter how hard I tried to escape, the one thing that never left me was the constant pain in my heart. I found myself becoming more and more disgusted by the notion of sex. Every aspect of it seemed rather revolting. It perplexed me how others could derive pleasure from it when everything I knew about it was utterly dreadful.

Instead of contacting Tyrone to explain what had happened, she shrewdly capitalized on the situation, preying on his sympathy.

Claiming she needed him. She mentioned having trouble sleeping due to horrible dreams about my biological father abusing her.

Hold up. Check the pot pies; when did this suddenly become about you? Do you not take into account the fact that I'm in pain and feeling completely worthless? *This lady is a piece of work!* She used a fucked-up situation to her advantage. I was blown back. And suddenly, as if it were a dreadful nightmare that kept repeating itself, they reconciled, and he returned to the house.

Initially, our mother was a first-shift warrior, but fate played its cards, and her hours were shuffled three weeks later. Meanwhile, Tyrone, in a twist of irony, landed a job that had him moonlighting on the second shift. That left us with one question: *who in the world would be keeping us now? This shit is becoming absurd.*

Papa Richard was blessed with a duo of witty teenage daughters. Dad reached out and asked if they would take care of us, and they happily agreed. Everything was incredibly fantastic. Playing outside was refreshing, and I had a great time making friends in my grandmother's neighborhood.

Jessie had the freedom to go wherever he pleased. I mentioned the whereabouts of my grandma's house, which coincidentally happened to be conveniently close to his father's house, just a mile away and a straight shot down 19th street. He would swing by every day to spend time with me, but his true motive, little did I know, was to fine-tune his latest scheme, which happened to be centered around a paper route.

We were scheduled to spend the weekend with Grandma, but she had a bowling match on Friday night and intended to stay the night before returning the next day. We'd already stayed with our aunts several times, so our plans were kept the same. I enjoyed visiting there since it was one of the few locations where I felt at ease and thought I was safe, but what exactly does "safe" mean?

Later that evening, we found ourselves enjoying some movies in my aunt's room. She was on the phone with her boyfriend, and my brother and I found it quite amusing to hear her discussing some rather explicit desires. We overheard her saying she wanted to suck his dick and have him nut on her titties so she could lick it off. I said, "Ugh, you'd think she'd stop now that she knew we were listening," but she continued with the bullshit. *Damn, she's a weirdo,* was my thought.

We always had an enjoyable time binging on movies until the tables turned and the movies started keeping an eye on us. I was having a dream as sweet as honey, only to be abruptly awakened. With a spring in my step, I leaped to my feet. I couldn't help but chuckle when I discovered that my aunt had stumbled upon an unorganized collection of toys scattered across the floor as she carried my sleeping sister to the couch.

I fell asleep once more. Feeling a tingling on my cheek, I assumed it was a fly and gently brushed my face. When I opened my eyes, my aunt was attempting to shove her pussy into my mouth. My lips were shut tighter than a drug dealer's final kilo of heroin. I was only half awake and had no idea what was going on, but I knew enough to push her ass up off me.

You will not make me a lesbian by default! This chick got me fucked up, and now she was about to get herself fucked up! I'm not eating any mother fucken pussy, now that's where I draw the line!

I pushed her so hard that she fell to the floor. I was more than ready to throw down. She jumped back into bed as if nothing had happened; now you got the fucken nerve to think you finna sleep peacefully? I stayed up all night wondering what she was going to do next. The more I thought about it, the more I wanted to leap out of bed, smack her like the Big Show, and reintroduce myself by saying, I'm Rick James Bitch!

I lay awake, wrestling with my thoughts, tossing and turning as I tried to navigate my peppered emotions. I must have drifted into slumber at some point because I suddenly woke up to the sound of Candice's footsteps echoing through the room and her greeting me with a less than-pleasant tone, saying, "Good morning." She began griping about spending the entire night alone on the couch and whining about being hungry.

As I carefully moved around, trying not to disturb anyone, I playfully reminded Candice to keep her voice down and promised I'd make a bowl of cereal for her. My brother was still asleep, but my annoying ass aunt was lying in bed, acting as if nothing had happened.

The way my aunt sprang out of bed, you'd think she was a human Jack-in-the-box. She exclaimed, "I got it, peanut," jumping to her feet and racing into the kitchen to whip up cereal for Candice. Trying to make small talk, she asked me, "Do you and Jessie have plans for today?"

I answered, "Yes, but I'm not sure what."

"I have five dollars on the dresser if you need any spare cash."

Oh, you honestly believe that five dollars will suffice to silence me. Girl FUCK YOU! Nevertheless, I was still determined to make the most of it. Even though it felt strange, it was far better than staying home. Apart from the fact that it was nasty as fuck, the only thing I was sure of was that I wasn't going to tell anyone what had happened. I was always to blame for whatever went wrong.

And what would I say? "Mom, she tried to put her pussy on me."

I'm sure her response would have been, "That's it, you're getting your ass beat!"

Chapter 7

The Scent of Fear

Jessie and I were making substantial progress with the crops. The hustle was flawless. I put the shit together, and he sold them. Jessie would get casket sharp and do his thing. The goal was to split the products evenly between Saturday and Sunday, allowing us to get to know our customers and observe our competitors' routines. Jessie would usually come to my grandma's once he sold out.

By eleven o'clock Saturday morning, Jessie was already at the door, enthusiastically declaring, "I sold everything except my Dick!"

I replied with a savvy remark, "Seems like we'll have the luxury of sleeping in tomorrow." He quickly began insisting that we needed more for tomorrow. I informed him that his idea was absurd and that it was impossible for us to transport a wagon filled with stolen items along a crowded street for nineteen blocks. *What the fuck are you thinking, bro?*

Jessie was on a paper chasing high and wouldn't take no for an answer. I was racking my brain, thinking, "No way, Jose!" I don't have the time or the means for any of this monkey-ball bullshit! However, I am a thinker. I knew that to talk Jessie down, I needed to make a damn good counteroffer.

I always carried my money with me; there was a store near my grandmother's house. I proposed killing two birds with one stone and purchasing veggies using our food stamps so we could rake in some cold, hard cash. I could tell Jessie was on the same wavelength by the twinkle in his eyes. We headed out to the store to get the veggies.

Jessie really impressed me. I looked up to Jessie because he had big dreams and never threw in the towel when faced with a challenge. When we returned to my grandmother's house, I cleaned the vegetables and packed them in his backpack. Once the vegetables were prepped and ready to go, we decided to take a little diversion to a neighboring park. The park was frequently packed with students from our school and some from a nearby seedy housing project that appeared to be just as bad as the Carter in New Jack City but without the crack. The park was in a pitiful state and evoked dread. The playground equipment was broken, and a lawsuit is waiting to happen. Even with the faulty equipment, we were too young to feel entitled; we made the best of what we had. Aside from the occasional fighting and shooting, the park was fun.

A large crowd awaited us as we approached, filled with excitement and vitality. I was initially hesitant and wanted to leave, but Jessie told me to get my punk ass in gear and stop acting so scared. We hurried towards the commotion, only to discover two boys getting it in. I was unfamiliar with their identity, but the crowd consistently talked about someone named D.

D was on top, wailing in on the boy like a hammer to a nail. However, the intensity of the altercation took an unexpected turn when a boy and a girl jumped into a fight; we later discovered they were the boy's siblings.

Jessie said, "Oh fuck that, that's my friend!" and fearlessly joined the fight. With a girl in the mix and Jessie always having my back, I couldn't help but get involved. We fought like cats and dogs until some grown-ups came and broke the fight up.

After things settled, D exclaimed, "Wow, who is she?" "That's my buddy," Jessie clarified.

D and Jessie were having a conversation when D suddenly turned to Jessie and asked, "Hey, is she a bit, you know, slow?

Damn, do you talk?"

I said, "Yes, mother fucker, you were talking, so I let you speak."

He exclaimed, "Oh, she's feisty; I think I'm in love." When the smoke cleared, it turned out that they were having a heated debate over a chain that mysteriously vanished following D's visit to the boy's house.

Jessie asked if he had taken it, and he responded sarcastically, "What kind of question is that? Indeed, I grabbed that motherfucker and sold it the following day." D joked that the chain and money were gone, and the boy received an ass whipping. As the sun set, I asked Jessie to walk me back to my grandmother's house, which he did. He promised to see me after he sold the crops the next day.

When we arrived home, my grandparents were waiting for us, and I was thrilled to see them. After the altercation, I ended up with a long scratch on my face, which made my grandmother curious about what had happened. I fibbed and claimed that I ran into a tree limb. I asked about the tournament where she had won first place. Her face lit up with joy as she proudly showcased her trophy and the impressive winning stroke. We ate dinner, bathed, and watched a movie.

After the movie, it was time to call it a night. I couldn't resist devising a witty scheme to get back at my aunt following the previous night's events. One thing I knew for sure was that I wouldn't utter a word about what had transpired for fear of becoming the scandal's focus. I also knew that hell would freeze over before she got away with it. It was business as usual when it was time for bed.

My aunt pretended everything was fine, laughing, chatting, pillow fighting, and then the infamous freaky talk to her boyfriend. I wasn't sure what to do when the lights dimmed, but I was determined to devise a plan.

Once everyone had drifted off into a peaceful slumber, I quietly lit our lamp. I settled onto the bed, pondering how to forge a connection with revenge. This Bitch tried to turn me into a lesbian; I mean, if that is your flavor, hay take a lick, but it wasn't the flavor I savored, and that shit didn't sit well with me. I would ensure she never dared to test me again in this life or the next.

Then it hit me like a ton of bricks: Since you want to act like a hot pussy whore, I'll treat you like one. I quickly grabbed the lamp

and placed the hot, fiery bulb between her legs. She jumped up and said,
"You little bitch!"

Having the advantage and a smug grin on my face. Boldly, I said, "Feel free to tell on me. The question is, what in the fuck are you going to say? Hey, I tried to shove my pussy in her mouth, and she shoved a
lightbulb between my legs? I think the fuck not!"

The smell of day-old tuna and burnt hair filled the room. I was so hot that a match set ten feet away from me would have ignited. She must have had severe burns because she lingered in the bathroom for hours. Even though I should have been scared, I slept soundly that night and awoke feeling great; she gave me some evil looks throughout the day but said nothing. I wished she had, but regardless, I had the upper hand.

As promised, Jessie arrived about eleven-thirty the following day; again, the crops had sold out after an hour and a half. Jessie immediately fell in love with the idea, realizing there was money to be made. He exclaimed, "We need more!" He began singing the Ojays' song "For the Love of Money" and doing a shimmy, jump, hop, pop, hip-rock, back and-forth dance.

I said, "First off, lose the dance niggah, it is not cool for a boy to be popping his ass, and secondly, if we take too much, the farmers will notice the crops are gone because they're in the middle of harvesting."

With a twinkle in his eye and visions of dollar signs dancing in his head, Jessie confidently announced his plan to visit the field not once, not twice, but three times next week, utterly unfazed by my worries about the possible dangers. I realized that arguing was pointless. And I also knew that greed had the ability to turn even the simplest situations into a tangled web of chaos.

We went to the park to spend time with D, knowing that my dad would pick us up shortly. As we began our game of hot potato, an unexpected high-pitched warbling noise suddenly filled the air. My stomach sank at the sound of my father's infamous whistle. My siblings and I grew familiar with that sound, a clear indication that it was time to head inside. I couldn't help but feel like a dog every time I heard it. Upon noticing that Jessie had also become familiar with the whistle, I said, "Welp, time to go; the dog whisperer is here."

Jessie said, "Come on, let me walk you back to your grandma's house." Jessie announced to D that he would be right back.

D glanced my way and said, "Hey, hold up a sec, let me holla at you for a minute."

I responded, "Who me?"

He replied, "Who else? Damn, she might be slow for real."

I walked over and said, "What's up?"

Channeling his inner Billy D Williams, he responded, "Thanks for the assist yesterday, but...umm, what's up with the digits?"

I remarked, "I really can't give my number to boys." I added, "However, I visit every other weekend. Let's kick it then."

"Cool," D remarked.

After the conversation with D, we returned to my grandma's house. Jessie suggested that I avoid D unless he was present. "He's not your superhero, and that tree is most certainly not a desirable choice for a snack."

I uttered, "Ok," as I inched closer to the house. My stomach churned with discomfort; nausea had taken hold of me. I strolled into the house, scooped up my stuff, dished out farewell hugs, and made a beeline for the car. Fuck! It's time to return to the hell hole, the dungeon of doom.

Jessie's clever strategy of maximizing the additional days to boost our crop intake yielded positive results for a few weeks. However, what goes up must eventually come down. Jessie casually asked if I could come outside today and lend a hand with the crops. I gave him a bewildered look, questioning his sanity; he added, "Hey, it is worth a shot." For shits and giggles, I asked my mom, and without hesitation, she said, "I don't care, get the fuck out of my face." *Gladly,* was my thought!

On my way to the field, I had a bad feeling. As we approached, I quietly said, "Hey, we shouldn't do this."

Jessie said, "Stop being so fucking scared!"

With an exaggerated eye roll and a playful lip smack, I approached the fence like a dumb ass. I said, "Look, I don't want to be out here all day; let's bring the wagon up to the fence, and we both fill the bags with produce so we can get the hell out of here!"

He yelled, "Bet!" in a cocky, confident tone.

After loading twice, I thought to myself*, All Right, that's plenty. Still, Jessie*, being his persistent self, insisted on getting me a watermelon and assured me he would be back. I grew restless after twenty minutes and followed him inside. Strolling through the field, I heard a strangely familiar sound. I couldn't figure out what was going on, but I knew the sound of bullshit when I heard it. Based on the commotion, it was clear that his goofy ass had been caught.

Peering through the cornfields, I heard the farmer calling Jessie a thief and threatening to teach him a lesson. Jessie was pinned against the fence, his feet suspended in mid-air, and the farmer's hand tightly gripped his neck. Jessie was yelling all kinds of foul-mouthed shit. "Put me down, you white pimple-picking mother fucker" he exclaimed. He had morphed into Redd Foxx right before my eyes. He probably used every racial slur you could imagine that day.

Jessie and I were dealt a hefty numerical disadvantage. It was a woman and two men versus two skinny kids from the ghetto. They could have lynched our black ass right there. I did not know what to do, but I knew I had to do something. I was hesitant to go for help because I was afraid of being blamed. *Fuck it, I will take my chances with the Farmer and the Dell versus my parents.*

I sprinted out of the stalks. "Please," I begged. "We are just kids trying to find our way." I must have caught the wife off guard because as I popped out of the bushes, she hurried over, windmilling a shovel, which scared me even more.

I slumped onto the ground, curled up in a ball, almost sure that I would shit my pants. I loudly screamed and said, "We come from the projects and don't have any food; he's not a bad kid. I know it's wrong, but we're hungry."

The other man screamed to the wife, "Don't hit her; it is a kid!"

The wife forcefully grabbed my arm and shouted, "You know, stealing is surely not the right thing to do."

I said, "I'm sorry; I realize it's wrong, but we didn't think you would notice since you had so much. Can we do anything to make up for it? I will get beaten if you take me home," I asked.

The wife yelled, "Johnny, let the child be. Let him go now."

I burst into tears when the farmer asked if this was my brother.

I said, "This is my best friend, and he was only trying to get me some watermelon." I didn't dare say, hey, the rest of the shit is on the other side of the fence.

"You are aware that this is theft," the farmer said.

"We did not consider it theft because most crops go to waste." I said, "I'm sorry, Sir," while bawling uncontrollably.

Jessie rushed over to hug me and reassure me that everything would be ok. The gesture must have touched the farmers' hearts because what came next was astounding.

"If my husband is on board," the wife replied, "We've been searching for help. If you two are up for lending a hand with the harvest, we'll ensure you have everything you need in exchange for your hard work."

I replied, "Yes, we will do that!" without asking Jessie. However, I needed her assistance, so I said under one condition. I pleaded with her to talk to my mom about the job, so she wouldn't think I was lying; otherwise, Jessie would have to oversee everything independently.

I gave her my address, and she agreed to contact my mother the next day. She said, "My name is Becky, by the way." Jessie and I introduced ourselves. We began our journey home once the formalities were out of the way.

Soon, as we managed to create some distance between us and the farmers, Jessie couldn't help but sarcastically comment, using his hand as a visor to shield his eyes from the blinding rays of the sun, "You're full of shit!"

I chuckled and responded, "What else could I do to save your funky ass? I had to come up with something." *But I had to know one thing.* I said, "Jessie, what's the deal with these pimple-picking honkies?" We made fun of each other the rest of the way home. I was glad we were safe, and I wasn't going to get my ass handed to me for stealing.

True to her word, Becky reached out to my mother. Remarkably, my mom approved, and we wasted no time getting started. Now that we had unrestricted access to the fields, we faced various options.

With an abundance of fresh fruits and vegetables at our fingertips, the possibilities were endless. The assortment of apples included a delightful blend of vibrant red, crisp green, and sunny yellow. The corn harvests were plentiful. Detasseling was quite a task; however, it was worth it, considering the decent amount of money we made.

To keep Papa Jack off my ass (literally). I told my mother I needed to work on Saturdays; she nodded without hesitation. I had the gift of gab and was also quite creative in arts and crafts. Why not spice up the bags and boost their worth, all while enjoying an inflow of profits?

I was always saving money, whereas Jessie preferred to spend it and buy expensive items. Nothing was wrong with it, but it drew unwanted attention if you ask my humble opinion. However, no one did, so I just shut up.

D and I grew closer on weekends, mostly discussing Jessie and school. He kept pestering me about how Jessie always managed to come up with the freshest gear and latest items. But one thing I did realize was the significance of silence!

As the phrase goes, in any black home, what happens in this house stays in this house! I felt the same way about our side hustle. Nonetheless, D couldn't get information from me, so he went straight to the source. Jessie told D everything and wanted to bring him into the hustle.

Jessie was always generous and kind; he would give his dirty drawls if someone would wear them. Letting this niggah in on the hustle didn't seem like a wise move. We had just got into the flow of things, and a three-way split seemed in no way attractive. Most importantly, I don't know this dude. Jessie thought that by using D, we could do more while working less. I tried to persuade him, but despite my better judgment, after an hour of back and forth, I reluctantly agreed.

Well, it seems my intuition was spot on. In the first week, D managed to swipe around fifteen hundred dollars' worth of tools. Jessie and I were pissed. We had always prided ourselves on dividing everything equally.

Would you believe that after jeopardizing our hustle, this Bitch-ass nigga had the audacity to give each of us a measly two hundred? Essentially telling us to suck his dick! Jessie and D had a heated disagreement. Jessie's point was that he brought him into the hustle so that he could make money rather than steal.

We could have lost our entire gig if the farmers suspected us, and he only gave us two hundred each. It wasn't about the cash but the boldness, the careless disregard for what we had at stake. Where is the irony in that bull shit?

Although I could understand where Jessie was coming from, I was also thinking I had already forewarned you against doing it in the first place. It never pays to let the right hand know what the left hand is up to, and you, indeed, don't want everyone in your business. And just like that, Jessie ousted that niggah from the kingdom.

Fortunately, the farmers never mentioned the missing equipment, and based on how they treated us, they had no suspicions about us.

D did them a favor. As a result, they purchased high-tech equipment, built a small shed, and secured everything.

In spite of the incident, Jessie couldn't resist harboring a lingering resentment towards D. However, he always managed to keep it concealed. Whenever Jessie swung by my grandparents' house, we would meet up with D at the park.

Eventually, Jessie grew tired of spending time with him, so we mostly stayed on my grandma's porch. Even though the boys' animosity appeared to be mutual, we had fun if we all happened to cross paths at the park by chance.

The conclusion of the season was fast approaching. It was getting close to the time to embark on another educational adventure. Jessie and I managed to accumulate around $5k in total. Jessie had already splurged on back-to-school clothes, proudly boasting about how stylish he would look for the upcoming school year.

He was always careful to keep his money nearby, never daring to leave it at home for fear that his mother or sister might get their hands on it. I tried to be the voice of reason, cautioning him about safeguarding his money. However, my concerns were frequently brushed off as nothing more than erroneous paranoia.

Upon completing the season, Ms. Becky expressed her gratitude for our hard work and guided us to a secluded area. There, she shared the exciting news that, due to our successful endeavors, we would be granted a small plot of land the following year to cultivate as we pleased. I was proud of our efforts, but more importantly, for the first time in my life, someone was proud of me.

I should have been over the moon, so I grinned from ear to ear, but my heart danced to a different beat. While Jessie was all giddy with excitement, I couldn't help but feel a bit down in the dumps when the farmers broke the news that the season had come to an end. I suddenly realized it was time to return to Papa Jack's, or as the locals affectionately called it, Predatorville.

Chapter 8

The Naked Truth Conceals a Vulnerable Spot

The week leading up to the return of school passed quickly. It was the last weekend before school started back up. I was excited since it seemed like the only time I could relax and hang out with my friends was at school. I overheard my mother and her sisters discussing going out and taking us to Papa Jack's this evening. I asked if I could go over to my cousin's house.

She responded, "No, you guys don't know how to act. Every weekend, one of the badass kids calls the club looking for their momma to snitch on each other."

After she hung up, I called my Grandma Wilma in a sneaky attempt to convince her to contact my mother and have her bring me over. I made up some flimsy excuses about it being the last weekend before school started. I added that if she made the call, I would scratch her scalp.

My mom bought it! Mission (motherfucking) accomplished. I was excited to see my granny. I convinced my grandma to let me tag along with my cousins, even though my mother wasn't thrilled about it. Grandma gave in, and I got my way!

My aunt and uncle had their fair share of disagreements, so it was another day in the never-ending family drama. The difference was they had advanced to weapons, sticks, bricks, and other shits! When the situation is so absurd that you're shooting pistols at each other in a park full of kids. Well, it seems like it's time to make a swift exit without any detours or pit stops. There's no need to worry about collecting any money along the way, head straight out.

Monday morning came crashing in like an unwelcome guest. Another thrilling day of education awaits. It was a delight to reunite with friends I hadn't seen all summer, and we were already buzzing with excitement as we began planning the first school dance of the year, "The Harvest Hoedown!" Tonae had her dress picked out; she was the stylish one of the group. I joined the student PTA because I loved to help decorate and plan events, not to mention it got me out of class early.

Now, let the dancing begin! After three exhausting weeks, The Harvest Hoedown was finally here. Not only was the dance filled with fun activities and lively music, but it was also decked out in festive fall decorations. From haystacks to donkey-shaped pinatas, the atmosphere was whimsical and entertaining, and let's remember the mouthwatering fair-themed food served, like delicious funnel cakes, fluffy cotton candy, and cheesy nachos. What a day to remember! Above all, my mother could not refuse because it happened during school hours.

Tonae was always in tight-fitted clothes, so the boys teased her that she was the hoe they would take down. Tonae and I loved dancing. Bianca was not a dancer, so she held our stuff while we danced. We had a great time at the welcome back-to-school party! Unfortunately, the enjoyment did not last long. I knew I had to go to Papa Jack's this weekend, so disaster was imminent.

Jessie walked me home from the dance and began discussing the paper route scheme. Nevertheless, I was interested this time. Working shielded me from all the stress at home.

He explained that the neighbor wanted him to deliver the newspaper in exchange for her paying him a few bucks every week. I asked myself why I would go from having a sizable weekly paycheck to kibbles and bits. *Duh, Fucking freedom!* I didn't care how much it paid; independence was priceless in my book, and *I* craved the taste of it.

In typical fashion, Jessie couldn't resist mentioning his interest in utilizing the mailbox again. With a clever twist, he revealed that the contents would be unveiled before his eyes by sliding the paper into the box. Every now and then, folks like to surprise others with cards filled with cold, hard cash. I blurted out, "Here we go again with this unnecessary bullshit!"

He shouted, "Ask your momma! We'll sort out the rest later, damn it!" I asked my mother. Yep, that avenue was a total flop; She turned down the offer in the blink of an eye. But whether I was involved or not, he started stealing packages, cards, and anything else he thought was worth taking from the mailbox.

As I spent more time at home, I saw that my parents' situation had not changed; instead, it seemed to be the drama equivalent of the Energizer Bunny. It just kept going and going and going. The insults reached new lows of degradation, and the fights escalated to a whole new level of intensity! Although I wasn't in trouble, I spent most of my days confined to my room. My mom was cooking in the kitchen when we got home, which could only mean one thing: she had plans for the night.

A few hours later, my mother called, "Y'all come eat." It seemed like everything she made had gravy on it; I detested gravy. It would be easy for someone to remove some chicken before adding the remaining pieces to the gravy, but that would have been too much like right. I voiced my concern, but of course, as the saying goes, "If you don't want this, you don't have to eat." *Don't threaten me with a good time, please.*

"Alright, I'm not eating, so I'll get to bed."

The barrettes flew out of my head as she forcefully swapped me in the back. "You little smart mouth Mother Fucker you going to eat every drop." *Wait, What?* I'm confused. I thought to myself, *what kind of mickey mouse bullshit is this? Did you give me a choice and then get upset because I don't want to eat your funky ass chicken wings?*

It didn't matter; we had a fourth chair, and it was only the three of us. I loaded the chicken wings towards the front of the chair so that you couldn't tell the difference. The following day, I planned to take them to school and throw them in the garbage. Fuck you and those nasty ass wings.

Kyle gave me a mischievous wink and said, "Momma, I need to go to the bathroom." Mom nonchalantly replied to go ahead. Kyle was about to go for the wings, but I had a gut feeling it wouldn't be the best idea, so I gently motioned for him to back off. Little did we know, our father was getting ready in the bathroom. Well, my intuition has always been quite sharp. Spot-on call if I do say so myself.

As soon as my brother caught sight of our dad, he tried to make a swift exit. Dad said, "Boi, you have the same thing I do. Come in here and use the restroom, little niggah." Kyle attempted to relieve himself, only to find himself unable to do so.

Without warning, a thunderous noise echoed through the house, startling us all. It was our father who knocked the shit out of Kyle. Dad was convinced that Kyle's claim of needing to use the bathroom was merely a ruse, an attempt to snoop on whatever he was doing in there. This assumption, however, left me puzzled. After all, how could we have known he was in the bathroom when we were gathered in the kitchen? Returning to the table, bloodied and with a busted lip, Kyle spilled the details of what had happened.

Unfazed by the unfolding events, my mother continued to pull clothes from the closet with a sense of urgency. The scene was all too familiar to me. It was 'Double Bubble' night at the club, a code for their late-night escapades. This would mean they'd be out until the wee hours, inadvertently allowing me to engage in hushed conversations with my friends through the window.

Tonae and Bianca convinced me to sneak out on this night, and I did! *Fuck it; here goes nothing.* We were having so much fun that it didn't matter if I got caught; I had become the DJ Khaled of ass beatings anyway, "And another one!"

We quickly returned to my house when we noticed the other parents' automobiles. I knew my folks would soon return. Tonae had to pee. She always had to fucken pee, and when she had to go, she had to go. I didn't want the boys to call her pissy pussy, so I let her in.

I had already changed back into my jammies and pulled my hair back. When I heard the key turn, my heart stopped. Damn, my

parents are home. I knew there would be problems in my Berney Mac Voice,
"trouble, trouble."

My mother always came in to check on us when she returned home from her Bill and Ted's excellent adventures at the bar. My room was directly across from the bathroom. Tonae and my mother collided in the hallway before she could reach my room. Tonae screamed, "Fuck!"

My mother yelled, "What are you doing in here?"

"I am sorry, Ms. Jennie Mae, I needed to use the restroom," Tonae explained.

"Get the fuck out of here!" exclaimed Mom. "I had to use the bathroom, my ass."

Tonae made a hasty exit, but not before discreetly mouthing the words "Sorry. I love you."

Once Tonae left, my mother beat me for what seemed like an eternity, and then my father stepped in; he hit me again, slapping me so hard I fell to the ground. The chaos woke my siblings; they watched helplessly in disbelief.

My brother cried, but Candice silently wept; she just stood there with her eyes fixated on my mom's every move as if she were about to make some motivating speech. *I have a dream that one day you, Punk Bitch's, will keep your hands to yourself. One day your funky ass heal will be struck and bruised like ours. Bitches and hoes will one day understand the wickedness of their ways and either stop or pay the piper.* My siblings were punished, but not nearly as severely as I was.

Can you imagine? After everything that happened, my mother had the audacity to bid me good night and say she loved me. To make matters worse, she decided to give her sisters a ring. The plot took an unexpected turn as my friend emerged from the bathroom, hastily fixing her clothes. We had boys in the house, ate all the munchies, and someone had been in her room. Lies, Lies, and More Lies!

Like, come on, none of that shit happened. I wanted to yell, "Hey, lookie here Bitch! I'm not sure what you've been smoking, dick, or dog
chow, but if you're going to tell the story, tell it, but don't lie."

We went from me violating the no-company rule to experiencing a dramatic soap opera-like situation reminiscent of Days of Our Lives with The Young and the Restless. I couldn't help but think that maybe she could use a vacation to the General Hospital for a little mental rejuvenation because it seemed like she was living in Another fucking World.

I was furious. I laid in bed thinking of ways to off their ass. My nose was running, but I was too afraid to get out of bed. I finally realized it was not running; my nose was bleeding. It went from a trickle to a full-fledged nosebleed. After thirty minutes, I got up and told my parents that my nose was bleeding and wouldn't stop, so they had to take me to the hospital.

I had bruises for days. When the hospital asked what happened, I gave my favorite excuse and said, "I was climbing a tree and fell." The
nurse said, "It must have been a high tree."

"Yes," I replied. "I was having a contest with my friends to see who could climb the fastest, and I fell backward."

She said, "OK, you have to be more careful." I thought, *what a dumb ass who in the fuck is letting their kids climb trees at 1:00 AM.*

The resentment was growing stronger and stronger in my heart against both of them, but more so my mother. How can you let this man do this to your child? Granted, I know it was wrong to have company when I wasn't supposed to, but it was not that fucken serious.

The next day, I went to school. I was so embarrassed, but all the kids were genuinely concerned. They asked if I was OK, and not one person made fun of the situation. I tried to play tough and say, "Yeah, that was nothing," but my body was so sore, I was welted up, my arms burned, and my nose periodically kept bleeding.

Tonae cried nonstop and apologized repeatedly. She showed me that day if I was hurting, she was hurting too, which made me love her even more. DHS was not common then; ultimately, it boiled down to

"Welcome to Ass Whippens are Us!"

Typically, following a beating, I would be placed on punishment, deprived of any form of entertainment, and confined to a dark room with no access to TV or phone. Heaven help me if I could stumble upon some sort of entertainment in this dreary room. I got my ass handed to me again; nothing meant nothing. If I breathed too loud, I was subject to get fucked up.

As the weekend approached, I couldn't help but anticipate my visit to Papa Jack's. Ms. Helen contacted me, seeking advice on what culinary masterpiece to create for our upcoming Saturday night feast. Without a doubt, I responded with, "Spaghetti."

Her spaghetti was terrific; I couldn't get enough of it. I also asked her if she could get some purple yarn and teach me how to crochet, which she happily agreed to. Ms. Helen and I had plenty of plans, and I was sure that as long as I stuck with her, he wouldn't be able to lay a finger on me. I was so wrong.

Friday arrived in the blink of an eye. Once we arrived, Papa Jack, like clockwork, was on his best behavior. The Saturday morning routine had begun. The aroma of homestyle breakfast filled the air; bacon, pancakes, eggs, and hot chocolate were all on the menu. I jumped out of bed, dressed, and hurried to the bathroom to brush my teeth, wash my face, and re-tie my hair into a ponytail. Ms. Helen said, "Good morning, Sleeping Beauty."

I responded, "Good morning, Grandma. It smells so good. Can I help set the table?"

As we discussed our upcoming plans, Helen and I couldn't resist sharing a few chuckles while having a great time in the kitchen. Suddenly, out of the blue, the Grim Reaper materialized to snatch them away. "I was thinking of taking the kids to the junkyard while

you ran errands," Papa Jack suggested with a mischievous grin. "You don't need
them trailing around and getting in your way."

Helen retorted, "Jack, cut it out with that silliness. I can't fathom why you believe an eleven-year-old child would be interested in exploring a junkyard; we have more exciting activities in mind. The kids are coming along with me."

I bowed my head in despair. Trying to comfort me, Grandma Helen tickled my side and said, "Don't worry; you're coming with me." I chuckled.

Papa Jack said, "Oh, you think this is a joke? Get into the room and see how funny it becomes after spending all day there." After she argued for fifteen or twenty minutes trying to defend me, he told her that I was his granddaughter and that he was free to do as he pleased with his grandchildren.

My siblings were watching cartoons in the living room. She called me out of the room to eat. After finishing my breakfast, she said, "Get your jacket; you're coming with me." Based on his hasty exit from the restroom, Papa Jack must have had a tracking device on my little Pussycat. He zoomed out and told me to return to the room.

Helen replied, "Don't worry about it, baby; I'll get the supplies for the project, and if I have to sit in the room with you while we work on it, we will get it done." Papa Jack's antics must have set off Helen's Spidey senses like an overcooked lasagna sets off a smoke alarm. I could see the wheels of suspicion turning in her eyes, each cog a new theory about what he was up to.

She gave a wink as sly as a fox in a hen house and sauntered off with the confidence of a runway model. She promised to return soon. I peeped her purse on the counter. Ms. Helen never left home without her pocketbook; leaving her purse was like a knight leaving his sword; it just didn't happen.

Helen could not have been more than a block away before he took me into his bedroom. He pushed me into the bed and yelled, "You want to show out? I'll show you how to show out." I leaped to my feet, sobbing. He gripped my neck and yelled, "I'm not playing with you; take off your shirt now." When I said no, he angrily erupted, "Do it now!" I barely had a chance to remove my shirt when he unexpectedly jammed his fingers inside of me.

With calculated intent, Helen deliberately left her wallet behind, a bait to lure out the monster she suspected him to be. I was unsure of how much she had witnessed, but it was enough to ignite a fire within her.

Bursting through the door, her voice echoed through the room, a thunderous roar of accusation and disgust, "You sick motherfucker, I knew it! Her words were laced with venom. "This is an innocent child; how dare you prey on her? You're nothing more than a predator, a sick bastard!"

Once filled with love, her eyes now blazed with a fury that could rival the sun. "I swear on my life," she vowed, her voice shaking with raw emotion, "if you dare to lay a finger on me or these children, I will not hesitate to gut you like a fish."

As she spoke, her hand reached out, gripping the handle of a butcher knife. The cold steel glinted ominously under the harsh kitchen light, a silent testament to her resolve. She was so petite, it shocked me, but she didn't back down. Not to mention, I had never heard her cuss.

After loading my sister, brother, and I into the car, along with a big ass suitcase, she drove us home. She explained to my parents what had happened, grabbed my hand, and said, "I'm sorry I didn't see it sooner. I love you." I hugged her; she held me so tight I knew it was goodbye. I never saw her again. Helen was one of the first people to ever stand up for me; I never got to thank her.

Meanwhile, back at the Ranch, it was my fault. "Now, who's going to watch y'all on the weekend?" That statement stuck with me forever.

Once again... Not let me take you to the doctor to see if you're ok... Not let me go over there and take care of business... Not let me call the cops... Not even let me talk to him to find out what happened.

Nothing! In no way was I vindicated. But I was happy that the truth had been revealed; she couldn't turn a blind eye if she tried; she knew exactly what was happening.

Whether we had a babysitter or not, my mother's activities remained the same. I took on the role of babysitter, and as a result, we enjoyed more quality time at home. One Saturday morning, she and my father had a big fight. After breakfast, my dad said, "Let's hit up the park!" but he put a dirty shirt on my sister.

Mom took it off and screamed, "Don't use my kids as a way to get out of the house." Dad quickly put it back on and punched the shit out of her.

He seized us with a sudden urgency and bolted as if the hounds of hell were on our heels. She was in hot pursuit, running like Jackie Joyner-Kersee in the race for an Olympic gold medal, only her baton was a butcher knife. We dove into the car, escaping her clutches by a hair's breadth, uncertainty clouding our minds. What the hell just happened?

She made a daring move, plunging the knife through the sunroof with an almost admirable precision. The air inside the car was electric with anticipation, our hearts pounding in our chests as we wondered if her vendetta was against him alone or if we were all in her line of fire.

We found ourselves huddled on the car floor, my teeth grinding with each violent stab she took at the roof. Fear and tears intermingled, streaming down our faces as we were caught in this surreal nightmare. Adding insult to injury, he was manhandling the car with such reckless disregard; like to hell with your children's safety. It was as if he was auditioning for the role of Evel Knievel's daredevil stunt double, challenging death at every sharp turn.

After being gone for a while, we arrived home, and Dad told us to go inside before he left. Her right eye was huge, nearly the size of a golf ball. Once again, their complete disregard for each other was on full display; this time, they didn't even consider the potential danger posed to us. Her stabbing and his reckless driving could have resulted in severe harm to all of us.

I had had enough. I said, "Mom, if you don't want to be with Dad, why don't you just dip, bounce, and run if you have to, but leave the man alone!" If looks could kill, I'd be chilling with the ancestors.

With the evilest look on the planet, she said, "Mind your own damn business and stay in a kid's place before I knock your teeth out of your mouth!" I had incredibly bright teeth and a captivating smile, so I followed her suggestion.

The stronger his disdain for her grew, the more intense his hatred towards me became. The beatings grew increasingly severe, with the reasons behind them becoming more and more absurd. I couldn't fathom the reason behind this agony, let alone why no one could help me. Miss Betty preached that God protected fools and babies; there was no protection for me, and I had bruises to prove it!

Despite the sizzling atmosphere at home, the school year kicked off with a bang. I made some fascinating new acquaintances, and my new teacher was delightful. Ah, at last, Friday has graced us with its presence. What a relief! As we exited the class, she nonchalantly mentioned that cursive writing would be introduced next week, emphasizing the importance of being prepared. I was filled with anticipation and eager to delve into the new subject.

It was Grandma Julie's weekend. D and I spent much of the weekend together because Jessie was heading out of town. We were laughing and telling jokes while seated on the swings. D had also heard about
Tonae getting caught in the house.

He described some of his family's troubles and urged me not to worry since it would only make me stronger. I attempted to reply, but before I could utter more than "thank you, D," he swiftly interrupted with "I got something for you" and handed me a chain. When I asked him where he got it, he replied, "Don't worry, your neck won't turn green!"

I chuckled, but I had no doubt he stole it from somewhere; he was a thug in the making. Taking hold of my hand and meeting my eyes directly, he murmured, "Can I ask you a question?"

"Oh, you mean, can you ask me something else? When you started
with can, you asked a question smart ass... Since I'm so slow!"

"Alright, you've got one up," D responded. I didn't return his gaze, but his labored breathing made my neck's hair stand on end, sending a shiver through my entire being. "Here goes the fundamental question:
Will you go with me?" he said.

I said, "Go where?"

D let out an exasperated sigh and dramatically rolled his eyes, "SLOW: slow is as slow does. Do you want to be my girl?" he remarked.

"Oh, I ain't never been anyone's girl," I replied.

"Well, you're mine now!" I paused as though his intense gaze had the power to see right through me. D playfully proposed the idea of keeping things private, but that didn't last very long.

I whispered, "OK, I guess, but don't spill the beans to Jessie."

He responded with, "Bet," like a confident gambler. Even though he was a thief and had nearly cost us our entire operation, I was comfortable. D was easy to talk to and confided in me about his problems with his mother, but I didn't trust him, so I listened more than I spoke. You would be surprised at how many secrets kids have to keep.

I told him I had to leave since it was getting dark. I didn't want to risk my little freedom. D said, "Well, since you're my girlfriend, you can't walk home alone." When we were in eyesight of my grandmother's house, he asked if he could get a kiss.

I boldly remarked, "Nigga please, no! Maybe next time."

He snapped back with, "Oh, you are playing hard to get. Can I have a hug?"

"Now, that I can do!" I retorted. That hug was indeed one of a kind. I never could have anticipated the sheer intensity of it all. That hug tugged at the jagged but piercing parts of my heart that had grown numb from previous heartbreaks. I felt safe for the first time in a long time. It was clear that D was a force to be reckoned with. An unmistakable aura of mischief surrounded him, yet his alluring charm captivated me.

With a sudden surge of energy and a surprising show of agility, he effortlessly dashed backwards as we neared my grandma's house. As he said his goodbyes, he couldn't help but throw in a clever comment, "I'll

see you next weekend; don't forget to stay sweet."

I exclaimed, "Boy, just don't spill the beans to Jessie!"

D Playfully shouted, "FUCK Jessie," while blowing me a kiss.

As I walked in, my aunt was sitting on the couch, braiding my sister Candace's hair. We were still exchanging wicked glares, but she didn't dare to say anything. It was quite the scene!

The rest of the weekend was as calm as a sleeping cat, and before we knew it, Sunday evening had snuck up on us like a mischievous ninja. Once home, I couldn't help but ponder what kind of reaction Jessie would have if he found out that D was my new boyfriend.

Chapter 9

The Point of No Return

Just another typical Monday morning: I dragged myself out of bed, wrestled my siblings into their clothes, and begrudgingly made my way to school. As soon as I walked in the door from school, my left cheek burned from the rapid smack on the side of my face that greeted me as I stepped through the door. I barely noticed the blood staining my shirt, but it didn't faze me one bit. This time, I managed to escape unscathed. I didn't shed a tear, and I didn't ponder the reasons; I simply headed to my room.

It seems that according to my mom's twisted logic, entering my room was seen as a confession of guilt. As soon as my mother entered the room, she wasted no time in unleashing her wrath upon me, hurling insults, calling me fast, and demanded immediate answers about D.

Confused, I blurted out, "A boy from my school." Although he didn't attend my school, I was determined to keep his proximity to Grandma Julie a secret. I had a feeling that if she found out, I wouldn't be able to return.

I couldn't help but wonder how she knew anything about D, but she quickly answered my question. She went on to say. "He's all on the radio, dedicating songs to you… 'Let's Get It On,' by Marvin Gaye. Oh, we're going to get it on all right." Now, I was left pondering the perplexing connection between any of that and myself. In reality, if I were at school I couldn't have caught wind of the dedication. Furthermore, if he was busy dedicating music to me, chances are he definitely wasn't at school.

As she paced back and forth, she said, "Yeah, I found your little note and chain," she aggressively broke the chain in half. I was so angry my gut told me to punch her ass in the throat, but I didn't, with tears streaming down my face. I stood there listening to her babble about how I probably had come on to Papa Jack and was a whore, rambling on about how "all these folks ain't just fucking with you for nothing." Inside, resentment was building. Hate is a terrible word to use, but I despised her.

I wanted to tell someone what was happening, but who would I tell? I was constantly reminded that kids are to be seen, not heard. If I told anyone, my mother would find out eventually, so what was the point? Since I was stuck there indefinitely, there was no use in making my life any more miserable than it already was.

The school year was going along smoothly; it was almost Christmas break. Even though everything was in disarray, I was academically a good student. I was excited about today's subject: cursive writing. The teacher explained the curriculum and how we would write the alphabet daily in cursive for two weeks; that was our only homework.

The teacher strolled through the maze of desks, her eyes sharp as a hawk's, dissecting our penmanship. When she arrived at my desk, she gasped and exclaimed, "You are writing with the incorrect hand!" Please use your right hand. I explained that I had trouble correcting the letters with my right hand and that it was better to use the left. She exuded kindness and offered to help at first, but the writing was terrible.

Despite my best efforts, she insisted on me redoing it. It became a repetitive routine day after day, except her demeanor grew more assertive. I had a stroke of genius and decided to start working from home. Mrs. Frankston swiftly caught on to my little charade of pulling it out of my book bag and pretending to write in class. Continuing her routine of walking down the rows, she paused in front of me and inquired. "Why are you sitting here?"

I replied, "I'm done." Her pupils were smaller than a pinhead. Her brow furrowed in concentration as she snatched my paper, rolled it into a ball, and then instructed me to do it again. I tried to explain, with an apology, that I was awkward using my right hand and that my left hand was easier to use.

Mrs. Frankston went to her desk and retrieved a ruler. She whacked my left hand with the ruler every time she saw me use it, but it was nothing compared to the Ike and Tina's greatest hits I received at home. Same routine on the following day. From the moment I stepped into the room, her eyes were locked on me, giving me an uncanny feeling that she was scrutinizing my every action.

The next day, I gave it a shot with my right hand first, trying to impress her, but I just couldn't quite get the hang of it. So, I kept going with my left, and let me tell you, this big back McQuack-looking bitch with a mysterious white crust in the corners of her mouth let out a scream that nearly made me jump out of my skin. "Didn't I already warn you about using that hand? Are you hard of hearing or just plain retarded?"

She sprinted to her desk and grabbed the ruler. The weather must have called for a spit tornado; spit was flying everywhere. She ranted, "Only evil people use their left hands because they are filthy."

I was pondering, "Hmm, you are the bitch foaming and frothing at the mouth, but I'm evil, OK." I got something for your ass. I put my head down, turned my eyelids inside out, raised both hands, and clenched my fingers toward my palms to make the letter C; my thumbs pointed inward. I screamed, "Rah!" Although some children screamed, the majority laughed.

She struck me with such force that the ruler cracked, and a hunk of wood lodged in my hand, leaking blood everywhere. I was sent to the nurse, and after speaking with her, I was directed to the principal's office. I had no idea what happened when they phoned my house, but I was promised a beating once we left the hospital.

The nurse in the hospital inquired about what had transpired.

When I gave my rendition, my mother yelled, "Stop lying!"

I cried out, "I'm not lying."

My father said, "I'm going up there tomorrow, and if they say anything other than what you're saying, I will beat yo' ass again for lying." True to his word, my father showed up at school the following day to play Inspector Gadget. He inquired with both the students and the teacher. Surprisingly, the teacher confessed to using a ruler to discipline me, claiming that using the left hand was wrong and we should only use our right hand.

He went off! He transformed into George Jefferson and launched a barrage of insults. He shouted out every racial slur he could think of. Dad had a Jerry curl, and I can assure you that the juice was splattered everywhere. With a firm grip on my arm, we dashed to the principal's office. When he arrived at the office, he continued his temper tantrum.

He screamed in the principal's face, "Motha fucker, if you or anyone else at this Motha fucking school touches my daughter again, I will fuck you up. Nobody will put their hands on my children." *Nobody except you, I presume*, was my thought, but I refrained from interrupting his strict rules and regulations. He screamed, "You better write it down, so you understand the scenario, Candice, Kyle, and this one; I'll uproot the entire fucking establishment for."

The principal's face was beet red. Dad pointed in his face and said, "You better look at my foot because the next time some shit like this happens, my foot and your ass will get really acquainted!" I was thinking, isn't that the pot calling the kettle black? I get my ass beat every day damn near. Nonetheless, the left hand was an acceptable form of penmanship after his outburst.

I began to undergo a transformation in my sense of self. I was filled with such intense anger and frustration that I had an overwhelming urge to engage in physical confrontation. The saying goes, "Hurt people hurt people," and it certainly proved to be accurate.

I began exhibiting disruptive behavior in class, defying the teacher's instructions, and engaging in conflicts with my peers. The noticeable shift in my behavior, at best, should have raised some red flags, but no one seemed to be paying attention.

Only one week remained in the school year before winter break. The only time I saw my friends because of the harsh weather was at school. It was too cold to be standing outside, chit-chatting in the cold, which made me feel even more alone.

The visits to Grandma Julie were far and few because my mother did not go out as often. I spoke with D whenever I could sneak on the phone. One of my friend's sisters went to the same school as him so we exchanged messages via her; she was the first UPS I had ever heard of.

On Friday, the school whipped up a delightful concoction of green cheese and strawberry caramel popcorn to get everyone in the Christmas spirit. Jessie asked if I planned on getting any popcorn today. I told him no, that I had left my money at home. The Christmas bags were priced at ten dollars. "I've got you covered," he quipped, passing me his popcorn ticket.

Every Friday, we were on the edge of our seats, eagerly anticipating the moment when the speaker would call out each class one by one to come pick up our popcorn. I casually plopped my ticket down on my desk like it was a VIP guest at a fancy party. A classmate's ticket had disappeared. The teachers assisted with the purchase of tickets, and because I did not go through the teacher, the student assumed I'd taken hers.

The student informed the teacher that I took it. Before doing any investigation, the teacher instructed me to give it to her. I said, "No, I don't have her ticket."

The teacher exclaimed, "You thief, you did not buy a ticket. Give her the ticket." I refused and tried to explain that Jessie had given me the ticket; without letting me get a word in, she continued to belittle me.

I said, "I don't have it."

Another classmate chimed in, "She had two tickets!" *Lies you tell Bitch!*

Despite her insistence on conducting a thorough search of my jacket, backpack, and pockets, much to her disappointment, she found nothing. She insisted that I take off my shoes in order to check if the ticket was hidden there. Once again, not guilty!

I found myself getting rather frustrated for a couple of reasons. Initially, I couldn't help but wonder why on earth I would need a ten-dollar popcorn ticket when I already had an abundance of money and food stamps. Get the fuck out of here. If I were going to indulge in popcorn thievery, it would only be of the finest, most delectable variety. Definitely not this cheap shit.

Why would anyone willingly make things more complicated over a few pieces of corn? That's certainly not the type of smoke I'm looking for. Furthermore, I am not someone who steals! Stealing is sure to attract unwanted attention to your doorstep!

Jessie was in a different class and, unfortunately, couldn't vouch for me. The teacher's voice boomed, demanding to know the whereabouts of the ticket. I shouted in response, "I don't have it!" Now way passed, pissed; this lady was irking my nerves. I pondered to myself, *If it is a problem you want, then I shall gladly oblige. Fuck it, here goes nothing!* Let's throw caution to the wind and see what happens! I effortlessly hurled the desk across the room, leaving a trail of awe in my wake.

There stood the bitch who said, I took her ticket. I kicked her to the ground, casually dropped the ticket to the floor, and yelled, "Go fetch." As the teacher bent down to help the girl up, I couldn't resist the urge to kick the teacher in the ass. She dramatically plummeted to the ground, flailing her arms while landing on all fours.

The whole class erupted in laughter as she soared over the girl. The teacher was a real heavyweight, literally! Every time she tried to stand up, I would kick her or push her back over, all while serenading her with the catchy Humpty Dumpty melody.

The students continued to laugh while the poor girl remained sprawled on the floor, now reduced to tears. But that wasn't good enough for me. With a firm grip on the chair, I gave my teacher a firm smack on the back. Whack! All at once, there was quiet. Crickets chirped.

Silence must have been a clue that I had gone too far. Well, all these ass clowns had gone too far, but when I do it, it's a problem. I would probably still be beating their ass, but fortunately, one of the janitors came in and grabbed me. I was kicking and screaming, calling her a fat bitch, Humpty Dumpty, and anything else I could think of down to the office, aka The Dungeon of Doom. I received a three-day suspension from school.

I anticipated a thorough beatdown. Nevertheless, it didn't faze me. As fate would have it, the ticket was eventually found in the bag. They never bothered to provide an explanation. I can't help but wonder if the cunning culprit managed to sneak it back into the bag amidst all the chaos or if she just happened to overlook it. Nonetheless, they paid the cost. The satisfaction of successfully defending myself outweighed the pain I would experience when I got home.

Once again, my parents were engrossed in their favorite pastime: the dramatic spectacle of domestic disputes. With the sun starting to beam, I got my siblings all set for school. Together, we strolled down the well-trodden path, their carefree chuckles providing a much-needed break from the gloomy atmosphere that awaited me back home.

When I got back, the house was so quiet it felt like it was echoing. The silence was broken only by the steady ticking of the clock and the steady thumping of my heart. Right after I got back, my mom took off for work, looking all worried. So now I'm left here all by myself to start serving my suspension without any interruptions! Seems like my father was keeping an eye on the house. He arrived shortly after Mom left.

He went straight into her room, hurling stuff around while muttering something about a resume. The way he acted had to be pretty important. He exited the room after about thirty minutes, saying, "Tell your mom I want my fucking resume," slammed the door, and left.

I told her what had transpired when she walked in on her lunch break. She yelled, "Fuck him and that resume! And I know he'll come back, so tell his hickey-wearing ass exactly what I said."

So, after rounding up the little troublemakers from school, Dad came in and asked if Mom had come home for lunch. I said, "Yes, and I told her what you said, and she told me to tell you, 'Forget about your resume.'"

"OK, everyone," he said calmly, "get your stuff; we're going sledding," I asked if I should bring my boots, and he agreed. Dad said, "Put on something warm," and hurriedly jotted down a note on a piece of paper; however, its contents were a mystery. Placing it on the table, we left.

We had a great time at the park, playing snowball fights and sledding for hours. Dad constructed an impressive fort on both sides while we made snowballs. Candice and I fought against him, and Kyle and we tore them up! When we started getting cold, he would whisk us away to the car, where he would make donuts in the parking lot until we were warm. This became a regular routine whenever we needed to warm up.

Eventually, Candace said, "I'm hungry and want to go home."

Dad said, "You will be OK." Another hour passed, and when I said I was ready to go home too, he said, "Your mother should be here shortly."

At that point, I understood something was wrong; we weren't just having fun in the park but being held hostage for the resume. The difficult-to-read note was most likely intended to accomplish this moment. Nevertheless, I'm certain he was not prepared for what unfolded next.

Mom must have sounded the alarm because, after five hours in the park, I saw my grandfather, grandmother, and uncles driving up in their trucks. My grandfather pointed his shotgun at my father's chest. He declared, "We can do this the easy way or the hard way, but you need to
get my grandchildren to one of these vehicles right now."

He took us to my grandpa's truck; we climbed in and drove home without incident. That seemed like the longest ride ever, but I knew it wouldn't end there. After a long day, we finally made it back home, scarfed down some food, scrubbed ourselves clean, and crashed into bed. Not a single word was uttered about what went down. We just hit the hay.

I awoke in the middle of the night to a huge bang; Dad had kicked the door in! They began fighting like cats and dogs. I lay awake, consoling Candace, wondering whether Kyle was OK; he had his own room. I was really crossing my fingers for the fighting to stop. *I mean, come on, it had been going on for hours! Can't we all just get along?* I'm not sure if it stopped or if, ultimately, I fell asleep.

When I woke up the next day, my mom was already awake. I hope it wasn't her fashion week outfit because she was rocking a seriously swollen eye. She kept quiet about what happened, but two large butcher knives were on the table, one of which was visibly bloodied. She put on her shades and left the house. I'm unsure where she went, but she was gone all day.

Jessie wasn't in school that day; we talked and joked on the phone. He told me about the Christmas packages he'd gotten, the money in the cards, and how it had become a lucrative business for him. He said, "Are you short on cash?"

"No, I am cool," I said. I couldn't spend my money without raising red flags, so I saved it. He inquired about my holiday plans, specifically if I would be spending them at Grandma Julie's. I mentioned to him that I was eagerly anticipating it, as I knew that our stay would be for at least one week. I wasn't sure about the timing of our visits to Grandma
Julie's, but Jessie would show up there every day.

I informed Jessie that I went to the park with D the last time I was over, and we had a fun time. He lost his temper and yelled, "I told you not to hang out with him because that nigga is grimy and cannot be trusted."

I said, "We only spent time at the park."

He replied, "I don't care if you hung out in a ditch; do not fuck with him outside of me."

I said, "All right, can we switch to a different topic?"

After a grueling six days, my father finally shows up, banging on the door like a madman. Given that his hand was bandaged, I assumed the
bloody knife I saw on the table was the culprit. When I opened the door, he asked, "What's going on? Where's your mom?"

I replied, "I don't know; she went with one of her friends."

He responded, "I know that she had you playing on the phone. You called my job."

I didn't even know where he worked, let alone what was happening.

"I did not call your job, and I haven't called anyone else."

He took off his belt, decorated with a lion's head, and began to hit me with it. This time, I was trying to get away from him, running, jumping, and wiggling. This niggah turned into Pootie Tang and WaDa-Tah'd my Ass. My foot got caught in the buckle, and instead of stopping, Dad gave it a strong tug, causing blood to spray everywhere. During the chaos, my mother arrived home for lunch. She
screamed, "What is going on? What is all this blood!"

He said, "She called the job saying you burned her ass with an iron." He was so wrapped up in his boomerang belt that he failed to notice I was bleeding.

I was crying uncontrollably, saying, "I did not, I did not!"

She responded, "Oh, you want to lie to people?" and started hitting me; however, the session was cut short when my foot began to bleed profusely.

After tending to my foot, we made our way to the hospital.

When everything was said and done, I needed several stitches and a blood transfusion, and I still didn't know what was going on. It appeared that they were unaware of the situation, as we later discovered that one of my aunt's boyfriends had become unhinged and tried to kidnap her, refusing to let her leave the house and burning her with an iron. It was her that snuck on the phone pleading for help.

Do you think anyone apologized? No, they went about their business as if nothing had happened. I was filled with anger and vowed to no longer tolerate their shit. I knew they'd never touch me in that way again without consequences. I had reached my limit and was done taking shit from anyone.

The following day, I was able to return to school. Bianca, Tonae, and Jessie came to pick us up from our house, and we walked to school together. Everyone was curious about my wrapped foot and my slight limp. I explained briefly what had happened and told them I did not want to discuss it anymore. One aspect of our friendship that I appreciated was that everyone respected boundaries. We did not pry or poke; we were in charge of our own narrative.

Bianca hugged me, saying, "I miss you, friend! Oh, Miss June has been bugging us about your whereabouts." Miss June was a woman who lived in the same projects as us and would give every child a piece of candy daily, but she also baked goodies, and I especially liked her brownies. Bianca told me to go over after school, which meant I'd have to bring my brother and sister, and we'd have to go there before we headed home because once we walked through the door, that was it.

The return to school was excellent; no one said anything to me, and I did not say anything to anyone else. I couldn't wait to reach Grandma Julie's house, where tranquility reigned supreme. With the break just around the corner, it was all I could think about.

Jessie walked me over to Miss June's. I arrived at the door to a cozy embrace. She stated, "God told me to tell you he sees your pain, and he will never leave you nor forsake you," adding, "You are destined for greatness." She mentioned that she was moving and wanted to say goodbye as she handed me a pan of brownies. Perhaps she believed saying goodbye with a batch of brownies would ease the pain, but it didn't.

I cried because I didn't want her to go; she was always so welcoming, and I felt safe for the brief moments we spent together every other day. She comforted me while wiping away my tears and reassured me that everything would be all right. Jessie hugged me and said, "I got you." While heading home, we discussed our winter break plans and Christmas wishes. I couldn't help but ponder if asking for a new family was breaking any rules.

After what felt like an eternity, winter break finally rolled around. My siblings and I chose to grace our dear grandmother with our presence for the entire week. My grandmother loved to bake, so we helped her out in the kitchen. Although grandmothers aren't supposed to have favorites, everyone knew Kyle was her top pick! It was all right because she still never made a difference.

Jessie decided to spice things up by unexpectedly showing up in the middle of the week. It was no shock to discover him up to his usual antics in my grandmother's neighborhood. Surprisingly, I was delighted to lay eyes on him despite my anticipation of our rendezvous being reserved for the weekend. He cleverly remarked, "Quite the impressive foot size you've got there, my friend. So, what's the size of those?"

"Oh, it's just as big as your head," I retorted. It turned out to be a side-splitting roast fest. Jessie always knew how to keep things entertaining.

My grandma's porch was the perfect spot for us to relax and enjoy the tunes of our neighbor, who happened to be a member of a well-known band. Grandma would whip up batches of cookies as we frolicked on the porch. During his stroll to the corner store, D noticed us and decided to join in on the conversation. After a couple of minutes, D said he'd be back in a bit; he had to make a quick trip to the store. He offered to hook me up with something, but I politely declined.

Jessie playfully remarked, "You certainly have an interesting approach! Instead of asking a girl if she wants anything, you should surprise her with a little something-something! Just so you know, she's a fan of Mountain Dew, orange Now and Laters, and any fruit except cantaloupe."

"You know a lot about my girl," D said under his breath. I gave him a sarcastic look, and D responded, "I'm just kidding. Yes, Jessie. She told me all about it last week!"

Jessie unleashed a scorching tirade on me the moment D disappeared from view. "I warned you about him for a reason. He's nothing but trouble." I reminded him that he was the one who introduced us. I couldn't help but wonder why he was spending so much time with someone he considered to be bad news.

Jessie was the one who first introduced me to the concept of keeping your enemies closer than your friends. I found myself rather puzzled. Well, aren't they supposed to be friends? A whirlwind of thoughts whizzed through my mind, pondering the perplexing notion of why he would help him fight if he didn't like him. However, my affection for Jessie was unwavering, and I was determined to avoid provoking his anger. He was one of the rare souls who truly grasped my essence, and the mere idea of losing him was unbearable.

I also knew I had to be the one to tell him I'd started dating D while he was away. I didn't want it thrown in his face or used against him; D understood how important it was for me to keep it a secret, but he kept dropping hints. The ideal time was now, but I couldn't bring myself to say anything.

Jessie kept a close eye on D when he returned. D had everything I liked in his bags. Jessie was aware something was going on, but he remained quiet. D started making petty remarks, hinting that it was more than friendship. He kept bringing up things we did when Jessie was away. But to make it official, he asked, "Where is the chain I gave you?" "My mother broke it after finding it and the note," I explained.

Jessie asked, "What did I miss? Are you writing letters and putting shackles on these girls, Nigga?"
D answered, "Yeah, that's my girl! And it is a chain, not handcuffs."

Jessie replied, "I beg to differ." I humbly lowered my head. Jessie raised an eyebrow and responded with a nonchalant, "OK," before he withdrew from the conversation.

I was itching to tell D to leave so we could discuss it, but truth be told, I found myself at a loss for words. Jessie wasn't just another person in my life; he held a special place as a brotherly figure. I knew he adored me and would bend backward just to ensure I was OK. Not once did he miss an opportunity to genuinely care for my well-being.

Jessie commented when D left, "I can't believe you agreed to go out with him. Accepting chains and shit!" I realized that it appeared as though it had cost me more than I gained, not to mention that he was dedicating songs on the radio, which my mother overheard, and I got the fuck beat out of me for something I did not know of.

He replied, "I can't tell you what to do, but I guarantee you'll be sorry. Any guy who smashes rocks through the window of an abandoned house is not the type of person you want." I asked what that meant and what it had to do with the matter at hand. Jessie replied, "Anyone willing to attract attention to themselves over a petty offense has a narrow mind."

I sat, thinking I'd made a terrible mistake. And as events continued to unfold, my worst fears were confirmed. Jessie gathered his things to leave. He mentioned that he would return on Friday with a little surprise for me. I also had something for him and couldn't wait to give it to him.

My grandfather had taken me to the mall to get the Pac-Man game; Jessie was a huge fan. I couldn't wait to see his face when I gave it to him. As Jessie hit the road, he left us with a parting remark that carried a hint of mischief, "I hope this D thing doesn't come back to bite you in the ass. I'm not mad at you; you're still my main apple scrapple!"

Jessie made good on his promise and returned on Friday. The weather was fantastic, so my aunt gave me the green light to play at the park. D and his friends were having a blast with a snowball fight. I jumped right in, but my excitement for the game quickly faded when I spotted Jessie heading to the park with two large blue and red sleds.

I raced down to meet him. "Hey, what are you doing with these sleds?"

He said, "I bought these for us for Christmas; I left another gift on your grandma's porch."

I responded, "Wow, I got you something, too."

He said, "Let's go have some fun."

I was in awe. He really paid attention when I jokingly mentioned to him that all I wanted for Christmas was a sled! I expressed my gratitude with a heartfelt "Thank you" and gave him the biggest hug.

D's irritated expression suggested an impending confrontation was brewing. He blurted out, "Jessie, why are you buying gifts for my girl?"

Jessie brushed him off, saying, "Man, watch out, bro."

D ordered me to return the sled to him, saying, "I can buy you whatever you want."

"No," I responded, "My friend bought it for me, and I don't need you to buy me anything; I have my own money!"

He said, "You heard what I said."

I struck a pose with confidence, hand on hip and feet firmly planted on the ground. Embracing my razor-sharp wit, I said, "I don't give a
fuck what you said, you heard what I said, and I didn't stutter. I said it, I meant it, and I ain't taking it back!"

D became even more agitated as the children giggled and made animated sounds like "ooh" and "aah." All that shit was cut short when I heard my father's whistle; I didn't need his shit on top of everything else. I sprinted back to my grandma's. Jessie arrived a few seconds later, carrying the sleds.

I couldn't help but notice a change in my father's demeanor. He seemed surprisingly cheerful. I was excited to show him my new sled, which Jessie had given me. Dad said, "Oh yeah, I'm going to have to watch out for Jessie over here buying these expensive gifts." I assumed we had to leave, but we didn't. As it turned out, Grandma was at the office, so he was just checking in to see how we were doing.

After my father had departed, I went to retrieve Jessie's gift. "Now, open your other gift," Jessie said as I returned to the porch.

I replied, "You go first; I want to see your face." He opened it slowly. I was happier than he was. I urged him to open it quickly.

He replied, "Calm down. It is not that serious." When he opened it, he smiled from ear to ear. "Let's go, Pac-Man! Now, open your second gift," he instructed.

Jessie packaged the gift nicely, and when I opened it, I found he had gotten me some boots. They were so cute, lined with fur on the inside and decorated with gold and red sparkles on the outside. According to him, they were a perfect match for the sled. I shouted, "Turkey! That's why you told me my feet were too big: all in the name of guaranteeing a perfect fit." We chuckled and savored the moment.

We still had roughly an hour of daylight. I asked Jessie if he wanted to return to the park, and he agreed. On the way down to the park, I asked if D had said anything else to him after I left. He said, "Nothing worth talking about, but be careful. I can guarantee he's got a trick or two hidden up his sleeve." I paid attention because the more time I spent with D, the more I realized he oozed of greed.

D was patiently waiting for us when we returned to the park. He came over to us immediately without a hint of negativity. He said, "I've been waiting for you to come back so I can say sorry."

I replied, "I accept your apology, but please don't act like that. Jealousy and control can really bring out the worst in people!"

D smirked at Jessie and mocked, "Who would be jealous of this dude? What a joke!" Jessie muttered something under his breath before walking away and engaging in conversation with some chicken head. After ten minutes of me and D talking, Jessie returned and said,

"OK, let me get you home."

D said, "I can walk her."

I said, "D, if people found out anything about you, it would derail my plans to visit my grandmother. My grandfather, who serves in the

Army, is heading off to Korea after the holidays." I went on to say, "My grandmother is throwing a celebration. It is too risky, but tomorrow I will be at the park. I will call you tonight if I can."

We walked away, and Jessie exclaimed, "You don't have to explain anything to that Niggah. Now hurry the fuck up so I can go deliver this package!"

I inquired, "What package?"

He shouted, "This dick!" I couldn't stop laughing. I was laughing so hard that I thought I would pee on myself.

I said, "I hope it falls off with your nasty self!"

When we got to the door, my grandmother said, "I was just about to walk over to the park and get you. It's getting late... Wait a minute, Jessie, I have something for you." My grandmother gave him a candy cane stocking filled with treats. After Jessie insisted, he had to go, I told him to give me a call when he got home.

True to his word, he called me, and we had a hysterical conversation on the phone while he played his game, discussing absolutely nothing of importance. But I couldn't help but ask, "Did you drop off that
Dick?"

He replied, "And you know it."

I chuckled and said, "You're nasty, and I hope you get crabs."

Jessie responded by saying, "But why are you in my business, and you fucking with this Sherlock Holmes-looking mother fucker?" We both laughed.

Jessie was leaving town to spend the rest of his vacation with his father, so I wouldn't see him again until we returned to school. After the competition vamoosed, the rest of the vacation went smoothly. D chilled the fuck out, and I enjoyed our conversation because he was easy to talk to. He handed me a card with two large peppermint sticks inside and another necklace for Christmas. Peppermint was one of my favorite candies.

"I could have gotten you a sled; I wish you would give that shit back; you don't need it."

I declared, "We're not going back to that subject, not to mention I can take anything my brother wants to give me."

He inserted, "He is only trying to rack up pussy points, and he is not your brother."

I assured him that there was no need for concern, not to mention Jessie wouldn't be returning for the remainder of the break. Even though I was tempted to fire back with a clever response, I decided to let his last comment be. Jessie had never tried to come on to me, so for him to say that was absurd.

The last few days of the week zoomed by, and in no time at all, we found ourselves back home, preparing to head back to school. I wasn't exactly thrilled about returning to school; the break felt way too short.

Chapter 10

The Cash Locomotive

The first day of classes flew by. Life was zooming by right before my very eyes. Believe it or not, at the tender age of eleven, I had already experienced the struggles of someone twice my age. The good news was that we didn't have to spend weekends at Papa Jack's house after his behavior was identified.

Still, it was a tough pill to swallow, no matter how much I came to terms with the situation. I would always have to look him in the eye on noteworthy occasions and holidays. Despite not being alone with him, each encounter was a constant reminder of a painful past that felt impossible to let go of, as if the same wound kept reopening before it had time to heal completely.

Again, in jeopardy of getting caught, Jessie had become impatient with his paper route and package stealing duties. Jessie said, "We gotta figure out how to keep the cash flow going until we can return to farming."

I replied, "You have enough money; sit down somewhere you're tripping."

Jessie functioned as if I was speaking a foreign language. He screamed, "What the fuck are you talking about?" Even though he didn't need the money, he was addicted to the hustle, and nothing could change it. Getting him to grasp my point felt impossible, so I shut up.

Nothing had changed with my parents. One minute, they were in love; the next, they weren't. I learned that when they broke up, she did her, and when she was ready for him to come home, Mom would always play the damsel in distress. "I need help with the kid's face, Ass," claiming one of us was showing out. When Dad came to punish us, all their issues would mysteriously vanish, and they'd be back together as if nothing had happened.

Their endless circle of break up to make up really pissed me off. What the hell was the point? All their fights were insane, but the last battle took the cake for me, no matter how hard I tried to forget. After being kidnapped and them mirroring Ali and Frazier's fight of the century, I still had one question buzzing around in my brain like a nagging ass fly; one thought refused to be swatted away: Did he ever get his fucking resume back?

Valentine's Day was drawing near, and while I continued talking to D whenever I got the chance, I found our conversations rather exhausting due to his constant babble about Jessie. D kept asking what we did with the money we received from the crops. My inner voice was itching to scream, "Mind your own fucking business! If you're so curious about
him, why not just go on a date with him?"

Then D asked, if my mother found the chain, why didn't she find my money? I told him I had stashed my cash and the extra necklace he had given me at my grandma's place. I only sported it on weekends to hide it from my mother's prying eyes. After enduring a barrage of never-ending questions, I brainstormed clever excuses to end the phone call. Two highlights were that I had to get my school stuff in order and "Here comes my mom, click!"

On the way to school the following day, Jessie commented, "We need to come up with some money. I'll keep delivering the newspaper, plus I'll also collect the monthly dues."

I said, "How does that put money in your pocket? Are you not going to turn it in?"

He laughed and explained, "Well, the paper costs forty bucks a month; she has sixty people on her paper route." He continued, scratching his head, "That's twenty-four hundred every month, and they give customers ninety days before sending a cancellation bill, by which time we'll be long gone." Jessie acted tongue-tied while laughing like a hyena, channeling his inner Porky Pig, and screamed,

"That's all folks! And that's where you come in," he said. "You'll dress nicely and present yourself to everyone, letting them know you're the new contact person."

I stated that for this to work, we must do it right. "We may face two challenges: one, my mother will likely say no, and second, the person you are doing this for does not even know me and will never feel comfortable allowing us to oversee such a hefty sum of money. Can you imagine little black kids showing up at people's doors to collect the monthly dues? We should brainstorm ideas and develop strategies to lock down our paper route and draw in our clientele."

Jessie proposed a plan. "After school, I'll talk to my cousin," he said, suggesting I should seek Grandmother Julie's assistance. He believed she might be able to persuade my parents. Taking his advice to heart, I did precisely that. To my disbelief, my parents agreed. Another plus was I could spend some of my money with a real job.

Jessie delivered on his promise. He had his cousin apply for the route since we were too young to do it ourselves. Jessie's latest idea was brilliant. We established a rapport with the customers. Jessie always delivered every paper on time despite the harsh weather.

Even amid snow or rain, he would make it a point to knock on the door and hand it to the customer to ensure the paper remained dry. *Now, that's what I call dedication!* We followed the rules for the rest of February and March, and everything went smoothly. I'd swing by once a week to say hello and see if the paper had arrived on time. I aimed to build a connection all in the name of ripping them the fuck off.

Word of mouth is a motherfucker. The customers told their friends about my excellent customer service and Jessie's timely delivery. Before long, we had eighty clients, bringing in thirty-two hundred dollars a month.

I discovered that when individuals perceive a child as having potential, they demonstrate increased compassion, so swindling them in should not be too hard. We had planned to engage our customers with exceptional service for the first three months, then cleverly exploit them for another three months before abruptly disappearing once they started receiving nonpayment letters in the mail. Their appreciation for our efforts was evident in the generous tips we received each month, amounting to a few hundred dollars.

Meanwhile, everything at school went smoothly until this girl randomly started making fun of me, just picking for no apparent rhyme or reason. It later dawned on me that Maurice was her boyfriend, and suddenly everything made sense. Maurice had been hitting on me for the last three school years. He was head over heels in love with me and made it known every time he saw me, but I didn't care for him, and I was already seeing D.

One day after school, Maurice asked for my phone number so we could study for a test on Friday. Since I couldn't give out my phone number, I agreed to grab his number and give him a call when I could.

After my mom went clubbing and my dad left for work the next night, I called Maurice. We must have discussed everything except the test material.

My mother had a lovely straw broom arranged on the wall as décor. I was lying in her bed, caking with this nigga, and flicking a lighter in the air. Suddenly, it ignited the broom, abruptly tumbling onto the bed.

I tried to put out the fire quickly, but it didn't work; it burned a hole in my mom's blanket. Just like that straw had wilted away from the flame. I knew without a doubt that my ass hair would get singed too. I hung up the phone quickly and started to rehearse my lie!

I was fully prepared for a well-whipped ass; I knew I had it coming this time. At first, I may have stretched the truth a bit, but eventually, I came clean and owned up to my bullshit. The crazy thing was I wasn't scared at all.

Mom said, "You little mother fucker, your always fucking with something every time I turn around. I'm tired of talking to you." I'm thinking, when was the last fucken time that we had a conversation.

"Take your ass to bed, and when you get out of school tomorrow, I am beating your ass!"

After a long day at school, I made a beeline for my room. She entered with a barrage of insults. I let her talk for a minute, but I was tired of hearing the shit; I stood there maintaining a steady gaze, and finally spoke up, "If you're going to do it, let's do it."

She replied, "Oh, you want to be smart?" the beating began. I was immune to the beatings. I winced but didn't cry; she eventually stopped, and I went to bed.

The next day, Maurice said, "It was nice talking to you the other night."

I replied, "I didn't realize you were so funny." We strolled to class and talked some more.

His girlfriend happened to be in the class and overheard our conversation. She asked, "Why are you talking to her? She's ugly."

I screamed, "Bitch, you got your people mixed up. Ya' Mama ugly," everybody laughed.

"Scrap your after-school plans," she replied with fiery determination. "I am going to teach you a lesson." *Hmm... So, when did this bitch start teaching?*

I said, "We ain't gotta wait until after school; we can bring the thunder right now!"

The teacher yelled, "Everyone quiet, take out your books right now!" We followed her orders. As class ended, the teacher reminded us that today was the last day to purchase Valentine's Day candy grams for tomorrow. I bought one for Jessie, Bianca, and Tonae.

Traditionally, Valentine's Day celebrations occurred in the classroom within the final hour of the school day. The teacher stated, "Wow, you've got quite the collection of candy grams this year." I was completely clueless about what she meant, but the teacher was spot on.

Maurice surprised me with a candy gram, six beautiful roses, and a delightful peppermint stick. Jessie, as always, got me one, while D went the extra mile and had our personal UPS purchase ten candy grams, each with a unique message. Out of all the messages I received, the one that struck a chord with me was from Jessie.

Maurice must have mistaken himself for Don Juan. He also gave his girlfriend a sizeable heart-shaped candy box and a teddy bear. The kids laughed and giggled, chanting Maurice got two girlfriends, Maurice got two girlfriends, he's a pimp. As I got up to sharpen my pencil, I replied, "Stop saying that; I'm not his girlfriend; I'm his friend," but this little bitch was enraged. She became furious after hearing the kids ridiculing her, approached my desk, and tore the candy gram to pieces.

Little girl! Please, tell me you did not just tear up my stuff. I ran over to her desk, grabbed the candy box, and threw it to the ground. I turned into Sammie Davis and tap danced all over that shit. The teacher hauled us both down to the office.

Ironically, instead of calling my parents, the principal told us we would both be suspended if it continued. Suspension would have made it more difficult for me to manage the paper route. I decided to end the madness since it wasn't worth it and would likely prevent me from seeing either of my grandmothers. I had way bigger fish to fry.

After reflecting on what I stood to lose, I apologized. Apparently, that must have indicated that I was scared. The next day in class, I got up and walked past her desk to turn in my homework. She mumbled,

"hoe,"

I said, "bitch" as I returned to my seat. She lived in the same complex as us and always walked home with the same bunch of girls, who would generally stroll behind us and talk shit. I let her talk since I knew what would happen if I got in trouble.

Three more weeks went by, and she just couldn't resist poking the bear. I always knew there would come a point where I couldn't just ignore things anymore. Just to play it safe, I decided to head home and spill the beans to my drama-filled momma about how this girl had been tormenting me for weeks on a daily basis.

I told her about the chocolates, the office, and everything else. I didn't leave any stone unturned. When I informed my mother, I wanted to fight her, she said, "You've got cousins for that, and I'm going to have them come over here and beat her ass." I told her I could fight for myself, but she insisted on calling my cousins.

The next day, like clockwork, she started fucking with me again, saying, "After school, I'm beating your ass." I went to the office and called my mom, giving her a heads up! When we left school, my mother, her sister, and my two cousins were waiting for us in front of the apartments.

My mother yelled, "Point her out!"

I answered, "There she is, but I can fight for myself."

She added, "Ok, if you get your ass whipped, prepare yourself for a two-for-one because I'm going to beat yo' ass again."

My mom looked me in the eyes and said, "You wanted the fight; get your ass over there and get to it," and that's all she had to say. I walked over and said, "What's up?"

The girl said, "What do you want to do?"

I said, "You are the one that wanted to fight; you said you would whip my ass, right?"

"The baddest one hit my hand," Tonae exclaimed as she jumped into the center.

I said, "Fuck the peanut butter and jelly. It is time to jam in this bitch!" I hit her in the face, and the fight was on; we were rolling all around in the snow. I ended up on top and put the skipity paps on that hoe! I stood up, and she took off running, saying she would get her mom.

"Go get your mama," my mom said, "and tell her we'll be right here waiting for her." We waited for her for almost twenty minutes, but she never returned.

My mom looked at me with wide eyes, completely unaware of my hidden left-right hook. That gave me the motivation I needed to ensure that, moving forward, I would fight, and no one would get any more fucken passes. My mom, with her usual fuckery said, "Well, if you can't do shit else, you can fight." She casually took a puff of her cigarette, flicked it into the snow, exhaled the smoke, and nonchalantly said, "Let's go."

Once back in school, the girl didn't say anything to me, but she was clawed up relatively well; she had scratches and bruises everywhere. I thought, *damn, I dug into her ass like a garden. Would you like peppers or cucumbers, ma'am?* I felt vindicated. The argument occurred outside the school grounds, so the school could not intervene. Still, they did speak with us about it and threatened to impose consequences if either party engaged in retaliation or caused disruptions within the school.

I was relieved that the fight had not caused me any problems. This was the first profitable month for Jessie and me to collect from the paper route, and I couldn't let anything stand in the way. We ended up with fifteen hundred each. It was unbelievable how they were giving up the money.

A few people wanted to pay with a check, so we had to turn that money in, but I told them if they paid with cash next month, they would get a ten-dollar discount. I was ok with the discount because it was free money. If they paid by check, we would not get anything.

Jessie was good at keeping secrets. He ensured our operation remained under lock and key, and I followed suit. We were like Bonnie and Clyde but without any romantic sparks flying between us.

Now that it was late spring and the weather had improved, we could finally go outside daily for recess. Unfortunately, my parents didn't share the same enthusiasm for change. Their arguments were relentless, and I always found myself caught in the crossfire, shouldering the blame for everything that went wrong. A few weeks before Memorial Day, the year was moving along.

My parents decided to go out for the night but insisted we clean up before bed. I accidentally neglected to wash a few dishes, not out of defiance but simply forgetfulness. As a result, Momma woke me up and didn't spare the rod. She was furious and demanded that I rewash everything in the house.

I assumed my mom's attitude throughout the day was due to my getting into trouble, but that was not the case. Dad had left early that morning and was out, Bobbie Browning (humping around). Mom was furious; she had been trying to contact him all day; we even went riding around looking for him. Later, when he finally arrived, the usual question of his whereabouts arose. "Where have you been?"

"Yes..."

"I was..."

"No, you weren't," wordplay exchange.

I couldn't understand why he was wearing a scarf around his neck when he walked in the door. It wasn't winter; this man was running around in eighty-five-degree heat, wearing a damn bandana around his neck. He may have desired a Western look; maybe that was the style. Who the fuck knew, and who the fuck cared. It didn't affect me at all. My mother had to have been thinking the same thing because when she yanked the bandana off his neck, hickeys were everywhere.

She screamed, "You want to wear a bandana, huh? Ok, bitch!" She wrapped the bandana around his neck and started strangling him. When my parents fought, my siblings and I would flee to our rooms. What a dramatic turn of events; just that fast it was on; he was yelling for our help yet again. His yellow jeans were so snug I could tell he only had forty-two cents in his pocket. He started flinging change around, ordering us to go to the pay phone and call the police.

His eyes rolled to the back of his head; I stayed there. I was too afraid to move. The neighbor called the cops because the noise was so loud. When the cops arrived, my parents were told that one of them would be arrested if they returned. So, one of them had to leave. That had to be music to my father's ears; he gladly raised his church finger and said, "I'll go." He likely had unfinished business elsewhere, possibly part two of his hickey spree.

My mom also departed from the house but returned after an hour. I'm not sure who she brought home with her, but what I do know is that it sounded like a Luke Skywalker video up in there! "Pop that pussy baby, pop that pussy baby!"

I wanted to yell, "Hey, shut the fuck up, I'm trying to sleep."

Candace, being older and more discerning, could empathize with my situation. She, too, experienced the unjust wrath of our parents, even for minor transgressions. Candice was smart and had a great passion for reading.

Our mother refused to sign her book reports, so I had to sign them for her to get her prize. Candace ended up signing her own one day. The teacher caught her. When the school called home, she got her ass torn up. You would think Mom would have signed the damn paper if she'd done the work.

She was high most of the time, and marijuana was not her only drug of choice. Our duties grew from tidying up the living room and bathroom to cleaning the entire house. There was always some shit brewing within our family.

My mom's sister was involved with Tyrone's brother. Their relationship was far from ideal. One day, an argument ensued, and all hell broke loose. When one of my aunts heard the escalating tension, she dialed the sisterhood line; her voice was a siren call of warning. The conversation was brief, using only the code word "this niggah done lost his mind."

Without a moment's hesitation, the sisterhood sprang into action. Car doors were slammed shut with urgency, and engines roared to life; bound by an unbreakable bond of love and duty, they raced towards my aunt's house, ready to face whatever lay ahead. Depending on who is recounting the tale, one of them received a thorough ass beaten. After they fought, my uncle thought shooting at my aunt would be a clever idea. My aunt had to make a daring escape through the window to ensure her safety.

Things had died down by the time everyone arrived. My mother was way past pissed about my aunt and uncle's fiery showdown. Once we arrived home, my mother quickly retreated to her room, emerging moments later transformed for a night out. Her eyes were hardened, and she left without a word, her silence more chilling than any argument.

Later that night, in the club, amidst the sea of dancing bodies and flashing lights, she spotted our father. He was laughing, having a good time, oblivious to the storm brewing in her. Suddenly, she confronted him, her hand connecting with his face in a swift, surprising slap, holding him responsible for his brother's actions. The altercation did not finish there. It overflowed out of the club, a secret family drama playing on the streets, intensifying with every lick they took. Then, like idiots, they returned home together!

They were filthy and mud caked as if they had been playing in a pig pen. Candice and I jumped up in the midst of the chaos. When my father saw us, he exclaimed, "Scrub this shit off my boots!" *Are you serious? Nigga please, I won't be doing any of that*! I went right back to bed.

Before calling it a night, they couldn't resist grabbing a bite to eat and continued their heated debate.

Our parents were still asleep when we woke up, so I asked my siblings to help me clean. I threw away the food that was on the table as well as some balled-up foil that was on top of the TV. After Kyle had taken out the trash and everything was back where it belonged, we began watching TV. When Mom awoke just after noon, she remarked on how lovely the house looked.

An hour later, she yelled, "Oh my god," in a panic, "What happened to that foil?" I explained that it was leftover food from the night before, and I did not think anyone would eat it, so I threw it away.

She took off running, trying to sort through the trash. I said, "We threw it in the trash; Kyle took the garbage out." She snatched him up by the collar and ran to the curbside dumpster. She was about to toss him in before seeing it empty.

Mom called us every name in the book and immediately jumped on the phone with her sisters like she was a mandatory reporter and told them what happened. "Would you believe these mother fucken kids threw my coke in the garbage?" My silly ass was sitting there thinking I hadn't seen any Coke cans; there wasn't any pop on the table; then it dawned on me I realized she was talking about cocaine.

It started to click. No wonder Mom and Dad acted like Ike Turner; they were on that narcotic. I knew what was next, so I entered her room and got the belt. She said, "Oh, you think this is a game?" and began punching me with her fist.

I stood there and ate all that shit without blinking an eye. I looked her in her eyes while she was doing it. Eventually, she stopped and told me to get my black ass in the room. I knew that crying gave her even more power, and I promised myself I would never give her the satisfaction of crying again.

We enjoyed outdoor recess the next day at school because the weather was finally cooperating. It had been raining all week, so it was a welcome change of pace. Although most of the playground was under construction, there was still lots of open space to play.

Tonae and I were playing hopscotch, and once I got to the top, Maurice started chasing after me. I laughed and said, "I told you to stay your ass away from me. I'd hate to have to dog-walk your little girlfriend again."

When the kids giggled, he yelled, "Shut up, let's race."

"Ok, but I'm going to win anyway, so what is the point," I said!

Tonae cried out, "On your marks, get set, GO!

I'm not sure what happened, but when I awoke, I was bleeding and on the ground. There was blood everywhere; I was terrified. My entire class was present, the teachers rushed over, and I could hear the sirens near.

When the nurse arrived, she placed something over my chest. I burst into tears because I had no idea what had happened. I couldn't figure it out. I was confused as to why I was bleeding and why I was on the ground. Tonae and Bianca, on the other hand, were right by my side the entire time.

Unbeknownst to me, construction workers were erecting a fence, which collapsed as I was racing past, severing the right top half of my breast. When the ambulance arrived, the nurse removed her hand, and I gazed down and saw flesh hanging out everywhere. I fainted, and I was in the hospital when I awoke.

The cut required stitches. I had to spend the night in the hospital for observation. My mother remained up all night with me, and it was one of the few times she was worried; she hugged me and promised me that everything would be fine.

Upon my return to school, every student welcomed me with get well soon cards. Except for Maurice's little girlfriends, each card was terrific. Hers had a lovely outside, but on the inside, it said, "Fuck you." I laughed and tossed it in the trash.

A gift bag filled with fruit, peppermint, a new edition cassette tape, and a teddy bear awaited me as I sat at my desk. Maurice remarked, "I'm sorry, I wanted to race. It's all my fault."

Gratefully, I accepted the bag from him, assuring him with a gentle smile, "Don't worry; it's not your fault." The school year was rapidly drawing to a close. The anticipation of summer vacation hung in the air like a sweet perfume.

Amid this end-of-year excitement, the school announced open auditions for a Disney play. This grand performance was set to be the grand finale of the academic year, a delightful spectacle to usher in the summer holidays.

By some stroke of luck, I found myself stepping into the role of Minnie Mouse. At the same time, Maurice, with his infectious enthusiasm, was perfectly cast as Mickey. After school each day, cast members were obligated to practice for the remainder of the year. Although it was supposed to be only an hour, I informed my mother it would be two hours to allow me more freedom. I sent D a note telling him I would be at my grandma's this weekend.

As we strolled back from school, Jessie asked if I would spend the weekend at my grandmother's place. When I said, "Yes, I am," he recommended that we pick up the money for the second month's paper route.

He stated, "Hey, listen up, business comes first. After that, you can see your little boyfriend!"

I pushed up against him, bumped him with my hip, and burst out singing. "Nobody knows the way you feel about it. Cause only you know; you can't leave it alone."

He said, "Let the Isley Brothers sing; you over here fucking up them people's song!" We laughed and talked about absolutely nothing for the rest of the trip home.

Chapter 11

Finding a Way Out

The ongoing tension in my parents' relationship had become the new normal. On our way home, I told Jessie I would collect the route money this weekend.

Jessie was flashier than ever, and no matter how much I fussed, he always carried the majority of his money with him. I was always fighting with him to find a good hiding place; it was too much money to carry around, not to mention how he would explain where he got it from if the wrong person discovered it. He said, "Don't worry, I got this."

My siblings and I arrived at Grandma's house earlier than expected, catching her by surprise during her afternoon nap. To make the process more efficient, I proactively collected payments from my paper route customers right away, ensuring that all payments were taken care of before the day was over, so I didn't have to hear Jessie's mouth.

I was delighted to learn that, once again, our quick service had received numerous compliments. I received all of the route money. Even better, individuals who utilized checks as a form of payment in the previous month had now chosen to use cash instead.

I finished up early, so D and I met at the park. Within a few minutes of my arrival, I spotted Jessie. "What's up?" D asked as Jessie strolled up to us.

"What's up, my man?" Jessie replied. Jessie had his book bag and basketball with him. I asked why he had brought the book bag. He explained, "I wanted to make sure you were at your grandmother's before I started throwing things on her porch."

I replied, "I told you she wouldn't mind at all." My grandmother was well known, and no one ever went near her home to steal anything.

I stated, "Oh, Jessie, I got all the route money, and nobody gave me a check." I handed his portion to him.

I couldn't help but notice D's razor-sharp observation skills; he was fully attentive to every detail. I didn't want D meddling in our affairs, so I cleverly informed D that Jessie needed to go to the restroom.

D said, "Oh, he needs to piss, huh? Well, he can do it on one of these trees." I pretended not to hear him. Jessie and I walked away. He appeared a bit antsy, so I assured him that I'd be back in a jiffy. The last thing I needed was D's envy. I accompanied Jessie as we headed back to my grandmother's house, carefully stashing the bag beneath the couch on the porch.

Upon our return to the park, D was nowhere to be found. However, his absence didn't dampen my spirits. I was still elated by our successful paper route and eager to share the news with Jessie. After talking about the paper route, we discussed the school play that was coming up.

Jessie often went with me to dress rehearsal and then walked me home. He responded, "Yo, I had no idea you could sing."

I answered, "Yeah, but I don't have much to sing about," and giggled.

"If all else fails," he said, "you can turn into a Blues singer because all they sing about is heartbreak and pain."

I responded, "Shut up."

He said, "No, seriously, you've been through a lot, and you're already a force to be reckoned with," and hugged me.

I was pleasantly surprised when I discovered Jessie held me in such high regard. I wasn't showered with affirmations or taught any valuable lessons about self-worth. No warm embraces or affectionate gestures were freely given, so I clung to it when I encountered something that felt truly authentic.

The way D kept behaving around Jessie started to irritate me, considering I never saw him as a potential romantic partner. Despite the imperfections, Jessie was familiar with me and my predicament and reassured me that everything would be all right.

After what seemed like an eternity, D still hadn't returned to the park. I mentioned to Jessie that I had to make a swift retreat to my grandmother's house due to my dreadful allergies that were acting up. He responded with a playful remark, "Come on, let's go. I'll be going to my father's place tomorrow, so it's time to head home and start getting my things in order."

When we arrived at my grandmother's house, Jessie's bag had vanished. He asked, "Where is my bag?"

I asked, "Didn't you put it under the couch?"

He responded, "Yes."

I said, "Well, let me check in the house; maybe my grandmother took it in there without knowing it was yours." The door was locked, indicating no one was home, but we would leave the back door unlocked if we went to the park. Candace and Kyle usually went with my aunts, so they didn't have to join me at the park.

I went through the back door to check for it, but it was not there. My heart dropped. Jessie was pissed. "I know D has my bag." He exclaimed.

I asked, "Why would you assume him of all people?"

He replied, "That the niggah was gone when we returned to the park, and he hadn't been back since. Every time you are over here, he
doesn't leave the park until you do. I'm heading to his house."

I replied, "I wish you wouldn't do that. We don't know who has the bag."

He stated, "You might not recognize it, but I do. He only wanted to fuck with you so he could learn how I move."

I said, "Wow, he can't just like me just because?"

He remarked, "Damn, you really are slow." I started crying. This was the first time Jessie, and I had a genuine disagreement.

With anger, he stormed off the porch. I ran after him. We got to the park, but D was not there. We went to his house; his mom said he had just left about twenty minutes ago. D's mom knew Jessie. Jessie asked if he could go to the bathroom, and she agreed. I was always told I wasn't allowed inside other people's houses, so I stayed outside to wait for Jessie.

After going to the restroom, he asked if he could leave a note for D, and she agreed. Jessie did not want to leave a message; he just wanted to enter the room. Jessie was carrying the backpack when he returned. He went on to say, "I'm beating his ass; my book bag was on that nigga bed." I couldn't say anything; the evidence was right before me. I could not deny it even if I wanted to.

Jessie said, "Come on, let me walk you back to your grandmother's house before you get in trouble," he offered. I cried the whole way home, and he responded, "I'm not sure what you're crying about; you still have all your money."

I told him, "That's why I told you not to carry your money around for things like this."

He stated, "No matter what I did, this niggah had no business touching my shit, and now we have an issue."

We stopped by the park on our way to my grandmother's house to see if anyone had seen D. Everyone said they hadn't seen him since earlier. When we got to my grandmother's house, Jessie was so upset that he refused to say goodbye.

I begged Jessie to wait. "I understand you are upset with me, but please give me a minute." I dashed into the house and grabbed my money.

When I asked how much it was, he said, "Two thousand."

I immediately counted it to him, and he responded, "No, I'm not taking your money."

I stated it was my fault, "You need it more than I do." Jessie assured me that he would be fine. I argued that I could not even spend my money right now.

He replied. "Taking an L comes with the territory. You worked just as hard as I did." Ultimately, I did not want anyone to be hurt. He said, "I am going to fuck him up, or he's going to fuck me up, but we're going
to fight. But believe me, I'm beating that ass."

Jessie said, "I have to go," and walked away. After closing the porch door, he reopened it and said, "I'll call you tomorrow." I said ok and smiled as I headed back inside.

After a few hours, I called D. I asked him why he took Jessie's money, and he tried to lie. I boldly stated, "You need to cut the shit, man.
Jessie got the bag off your bed."

D said, "Wait, hold on." I heard a scream, "Fuck!" He came back on the phone and said, "Hello?"

I said, "Yes, I'm here. Why would you do that to him? In fact, why would you do that to me? You asked me plenty of questions about Jessie and his money. Why would you take his money if you were such good friends?"

He said, "I don't care who it is, I'm in a situation right now, and I have to come up with this money; people are talking about killing my
Mama, so I have to do what I have to do."

"Why would they want to kill your mother? Are you going to rob me too?"

He replied, "No, I would never do that to you."

"Well, robbing Jessie is the same as stealing from me!"

He said, "No, it isn't. I would never have had to do something like this if they weren't threatening my mother."

I couldn't bear to continue hearing his absurd babble. I casually mentioned, "I'll give you a call tomorrow." I concocted a clever tale about my aunt's urgent need for the phone.

I was caught in a bind. I tried to ignore the dagger that was tied to his funky ass secret. I told myself that anticipating casualties in war was a reason for the betrayal, and with everything on the line for him, his desperation made perfect sense. But that's nowhere near a plausible argument, niggah, you went against the grain!

That's when I discovered I cared much more for Jessie than I imagined. "If you fuck with one of us, you fuck with all of us," my mother and her sisters would tell us, and that's precisely how I felt. I didn't know what should be done, but somehow, I understood exactly what would be done!

I called Jessie. I feared he wouldn't say anything to me, but he did. He quickly apologized and stated that he was upset. He grew enraged and silent when I informed him about my talk with D. After a small wait, I said, "Hello?"

He replied, "Sure, as my name is Jessie, I am fucking him up!"

I responded, "And I'm helping."

He answered, "I don't need your help; I've always had it, but the fact that you want to says a lot."

I begged, "Please come get this money before going to your father's."

He said, "I don't need it; you know we'll get it back at the end of the month." He added, "Plus, I still have money. I paid attention to what you said. I was so angry when we discussed it that I forgot I only had eight hundred in the bag and put the money you gave me in my pocket."

I replied, "Well, even though the amount is small, I still want to pay for it because I feel responsible."

"No," he responded, "that comes with the territory. I've got to charge that to the game." I was grinning from ear to ear because, despite his pushback, he was listening and trusted me enough to heed my suggestion.

My grandma told me it was time to hang up the phone, so I told Jessie I would talk to him on Monday. When Saturday afternoon rolled around, my granny asked if I was heading to the park. Jessie was planning to go to his father's place, so I told her, "No," and replied, "I'm just going to stay indoors." A little after noon, there was a knock at my grandmother's door. It was Jessie.

"What are you doing here?" I asked. Little did I know, Jessie was so angry that he blew off his father's visit.

He wore a jogging pantsuit, a t-shirt, a blue hat, and matching shoes. Even when he wasn't being flamboyant, he dressed head to toe. The issue was that Jessie didn't have any jewelry on. Jessie never left the house without his watch, and even though he wasn't keeping track of time that day, I was, and I knew exactly what time it was. In the words
of Michael Buffer, "Let's get ready to rumble!"

Jessie grabbed my arm and said, "Let's go to the park."

I answered, "Bet." The way he was dressed and the fact he had no watch on, I knew Jessie was serious.

Jessie's expression turned ice cold as soon as he caught sight of D. Without saying a word, he continued charging straight toward him, with me right by his side. D got so caught up in telling his story he was unaware we were on his ass. D stopped speaking in the middle of a sentence when we were all face to face.

Jessie firmly stated, "I'm not going to play with you."

"Are you riding with this niggah?" D's puzzled gaze landed on me.

I said, "Hell yeah." Our friendship Cadillac has been running full throttle since we were five years old, and we have never once run out of gas. I yelled, "Fuck the dumb shit," and knocked the hell out of him while screaming, "You bitch ass niggah!" Jessie pushed me aside and went Wreck it Ralph on his ass!

Jessie was hammering the shit out of D; they were fighting like cats and dogs. Don't get it twisted; he was up against some stiff competition. D gave him a run for his money. However, the battle was over when Jessie destroyed his glasses; D was stumbling around swinging but not making any connections.

At the same time as the fight, a baseball game was being played. The coach ran over to break the boys up. D was covered with blood. Everyone seemed confused by what was happening, saying things like, "I thought they were friends," which I also assumed. D left after the fight, and Jessie and I returned to my grandmother's house. However, it would not be the end of it!

Jessie's mouth was bleeding, so I grabbed him a towel and some ice; he was beaming from ear to ear. "Why are you smiling?" I asked.

"I told you I was going to get that nigga," he replied.

I said, "And you sure did." We re-enacted the entire conflict, blow by blow until Jessie's sister arrived to pick him up. Once back at his place, we had a quick phone conversation. He stated he was tired and about to shower but promised to call me the next day.

I immediately called D. He said, "What the fuck do you want?"

I said, "I was checking on you. It's beyond me why you used me as a pawn to get close to Jessie."

He stated, "I didn't use you to get next to Jessie. I didn't want him in my girl's face, and he was always trying to be funny, so I robbed him."

I said, "Well, you lost your girl and your friend; I quit you!" I added, "I thought you said someone was going to kill your Mama with your lying ass."

He said, "It doesn't matter because you're done with me; I only told you that because I didn't want you to leave. Fuck you!"

I replied, "Oh, fuck me, huh? I must say, I find it quite distasteful when individuals take advantage of their so-called friends to get ahead.
It's a quality that is not very attractive. I'm done with you."

He replied, "Well, you'll probably be a slut anyway."

I said, "Kiss my ass, punk; that's why you got beat the fuck up!" and hung up.

"Watch your mouth," my aunt warned. "You're too young to be cursing like that." *How fortunate you alert me to mind my mouth after you gather your ammunition.*

I had the right mind to say, who in the entire fuck are you talking to? Instead, I murmured, "Girl, go to hell and do it moving!"

Nevertheless, during this entire time, she was connecting the dots with her ear-hustling ass. My aunt shrewdly remarked, "I heard that. And oh, by the way, I've got some juicy gossip for you! One of my friends spilled all the beans about what went down at the park. I'll be sure to provide your mother with all the details. Let's see who can laugh the longest!"

My aunt told my mother everything that had happened between Jessie and D; she sounded like she had diarrhea of the mouth the way shit was running out her lips! She also told my mom D was my boyfriend and where he lived.

"That's why you always want to come over here," Mom remarked; "wait until we get home!" When I arrived home, Mom began ranting and screaming about how I lied about him attending my school and how he couldn't possibly live down there and go to the same school.

I paid attention to everything, so I knew from the beginning that two things were happening. First, my dad would always get us; my mom would only get us if they were into it. Second, I could tell she was high because she usually had this glossy eye look. I didn't say a word; I just let her ramble; she was having a whole conversation with herself.

"Yep, I knew all along that there was a reason your hot ass wanted to go down there. You think your slick hu, I don't know anything right, shit, ain't nobody stupid."

The phone rang in the middle of her speech; it was her sister's, and they were on a three-way call. I heard them discussing my mother's relocation. I heard her say that she had applied for low-income housing and that her name was number three on the waiting list. My dad came out of the room with his duffle bag. Yes, they were fighting; he had packed up his shit again.

"Yeah, excuse me, I'm not trying to fuck up y'all little sisterly ménage à trois but me or my kids are not moving out of state," he said after overhearing the conversation. He slammed the door and left.

She acted like he hadn't said a damn thing. I thought, *wait, what? These are the only friends I have.* Out of state, no, this can't be happening. We began in Pre-K and are now preparing to enter Junior High School. I had no idea what was happening; I ran to my room and remained there for hours, fearing the unknown. Not to mention, I wasn't sure if she was going to walk in and kick my teeth down my throat because of what my aunt had told her.

The paper route was going well, and we were still rehearsing the Disney play. As I twirled away from Mickey in the Disney closing scene, I had to pretend I would kiss him. Saying, "Oh, Mickey, you're so pretty, don't you understand you take me by the heart, not the lips!" I knew every sentence by heart, but the spin needed to be revised. I kept offering him my left hand even though I was supposed to extend my right, but I was adamant that everything would work out.

I was still trying to work out the details of their most recent argument. Whatever it was, it had to be intense because he'd moved out and was looking for a new place. Everyone except for them realized the relationship had ended long ago.

They fought over frivolous bullshit. One night, my father banged on the bathroom door, claiming she took too long to wipe her ass. However, the dumb shit went both ways. My mother accused my father of eating food from another bitch's house and getting gas. I mean, seriously, how do you phrase your theory?

"I know Vicki Ann likes garlic, and I noticed her recklessly eyeballing you at the grocery store before you hurried to aisle seven to get the bitch's phone number. Now you got your funky ass in here farting, smelling like a shit mill."

The nonsense was driving me crazy; Get the fuck out of here! News Flash, the shit is over, and it's ok for one of you dimwits to be an adult and walk the fuck away. But no, the story continues, and I'm positively sure they had a sequel coming.

They were both moving strangely. My mother mentioned that we would see a male acquaintance this weekend. How come? For the fuck what? The only men we saw were entering and exiting her bedroom, and they never said anything to us. Wam, Bam, Thank you, Ma'am.

My mother picked us up from school. When I asked her where we were going, she said, "To see my friend." Once we got there, we discovered it was a man named Peter. She told us that we would be spending the weekend at his place. He seemed to have a calm demeanor. He was holding her around her waist and kissed her on the neck.

What in the holy hell kind of friend is that? Me and Jessie would never do no shit like that. Candice exclaimed, "Yuck!"

My mother gave her a look that said, "Shut the hell up before I beat your ass."

"Jennie," he stated. "Do you want to stay here, or would you and the kids like to come with me?"

"I need to run to the supermarket."

He said better yet, "Nope, come on, I want the kids to pick out a few things. I want to make sure they are comfortable."

During our shopping trip, he went the whole nine yards and spoiled us rotten. Everything was running like clockwork. He wasted no time trying to woo my mother in the kitchen, channeling his inner Betty Crocker to whip up a meal for us. My mom was beaming from ear to ear and looked happy. She was beautiful when she smiled.

After dinner, Kyle and I were on the porch enjoying ourselves. Candice was sleeping. It was so peaceful I thought, *Wow, is this how real families operate!* But then, ten minutes later, the shit show started!

My mother and Peter were watching a movie together. A woman approached the screen door while we were playing on the porch. Thank God the screen door was locked. She started with the 'Enquiring minds want to know' speech.

"Who are you?" she asked.

"Who are you?" I responded.

"What's your mom's name?" she asked.

"What's your mom's name?" I answered.

"Well, could you go get your mom?" she asked. I said, "Now that I can do!" *It would have been most helpful if she had started there.*

"Mom," I began as I stepped inside, "there's a woman out here asking for you."

Peter responded, "A woman?" My mother rose up; Peter said, "I got it, baby." Peter and Mom exchanged a few words. I snatched up Kyle and led him back inside. No sooner than we bent the corner, the woman and Peter started arguing.

I overheard him say, "You should go; you're disrespecting my guest."

"Nigga, you've been lying and pretending like it's just you and me, and you over here playing daddy to some other bitch's kids," the woman shouted. There was a loud bang.

My mom ran out to see what was happening. "Oh, hell no!" she screamed.

As she tried to escape out the door, Peter held her and said, "I got

it, Jennie. It's cool. I got it. Just go into the house."

"I've got it, my ass." My mother yelled. Her demeanor was anything but calm when she returned inside. My mother said, "Y'all stay here, and you better not move." She bolted out of the back door. I told my brother the same thing: stay here and don't come out. I ran out the back after my mom. I got to the front, and my mom was on that woman like white on rice.

She was sitting on top of her, beating the living daylights out of her; she tore her a new ass. Peter grabbed my mother and pleaded, "Baby, please just go into the house." The bang we heard was her busting out my mom's car window.

When she returned to the house, she gathered our belongings and said, "I don't have time for this. I'm already in a crazy situation; I'll be damned if I go into another. Please don't call me anymore."

Kyle said, "Sir, can we have the snacks?"

My mom said, "Boy fuck them, snacks! Let's go, Dammit."

The man passed the bag to Kyle as we walked out the door. My mom snatched it, threw the bag on the ground, and told us to get in the car. On her final trip into the house, I jumped out of the car and grabbed the snack bag. Those snacks hadn't done anything to anybody, and I saw no reason to forsake them.

When we got in the car, we discovered that the back seat was a blanket of broken glass, so we were forced to sit in the front. My mother turned to Peter as she drove off and said, "You owe me a window."

Peter did not want any smoke; the window was fixed the following day.

Mom could not wait to call her sisters when we arrived home. She kept talking to her sisters increasingly, and we were talking to our dad less and less. I realized it was the end for my parents because they were both moving weirdly.

It was Monday already! On our walk home, we discovered that only twenty-one days remained in the school year. We discussed what it would be like to attend a new school and imagined ourselves all in the same class. Bianca was first to notice that whenever the topic came up, I would inevitably become silent and withdrawn. She questioned, "Are you scared to go to junior high?" "No, why would you say that?" I responded.

She answered, "You get very quiet when discussing it."

I said, "No, *now is as good a time as any*. "My mother wants to move out of state, so we may not be able to attend school together."

Tonae said, "Are you serious?"

"Yes," I replied. I knew Jessie's father lived in that city, so if Jessie paid a visit to his father, depending on the location, I might be able to see him.

On that very day, Tonae, Bianca, and I pledged to stick together and not let anything stand in our way. We agreed to swap contact information the following day.

On our walk to school the next day, Tonae mentioned that she had seen a moving truck at Bianca's house. Our curiosity was piqued, so we decided to investigate after school. To our surprise, the house was completely vacant, which explains why she wasn't at school. I was worried about where she had gone. The idea of our trio being separated seemed surreal. A rush of memories flooded back all at once.

As I strolled back, tears began streaming down my face. I had a strong connection with all my friends, but Bianca and I were especially close. We completed each other's sentences. We were both Virgos, with our birthdays barely a week apart. We were literally two peas in a pod.

She was a compassionate soul, always willing to lend an ear, and we kept each other's secrets under lock and key. Her witty sense of humor was a perfect match for mine. She was as empathetic and encouraging as they came, regardless of any differing opinions.

Tonae was all those things; except she had developed a carefree attitude of accepting things as they were and moving forward without dwelling on them. Although the advice was helpful, I preferred to address the issue myself instead of leaving it unresolved; otherwise, it would be like a monkey on my back and drive me batshit crazy.

Word spreads quickly. Our father arrived at school and separately pulled Kyle and me out of class. He asked if we went to a man's house this weekend. I answered, "Yes, but we didn't stay." He asked if my mom
and a lady got into a fight, to which I responded, "Yes."

He said, "OK, love you, go back to class." Kyle and I exchanged stories on the walk home. We told our mother what had transpired. She went off on us and said we had no right to tell him anything!

Five minutes into her tongue-lashing, our dad made his grand entry. He rushed nose to nose with my mother, shaking his finger toward her face. His voice was stern and laced with an I will fuck you up tone: "I specifically told you not to have any dudes around my kids? "You're playing with fire, and bitch you're about to get burnt." "Well, only two of them are yours!" she said. He responded, "Oh, Bitch, is that the game we're playing?"

She replied, "Well, your daughter, as she calls herself, has a boyfriend over by your mom's, and they have to go over there this weekend, so you better talk to her or beat her ass." It was that instant that I understood it was over; my parents were finished.

He walked over to her; they were nose to nose, and he screamed, "That's your daughter! You talk to her about it or beat her ass; I ain't got shit to say." When he opened the door, he hit the screen door so hard that the glass violently shattered.

It was the weekend. Jessie cautioned me about going to the park alone on our walk home. He had a hunch that D would try to hurt me. "This weekend, I might be going to see my grandmother, but if not, I'll be over to hang out at your grandma's," Jessie continued, "Hey, black ass, pay attention! Say it with me. 'Remain clear of the park!' In other words, don't take your ass over there."

I grinned and replied, "He won't do anything."

"I know because you won't be going without me," he said.

Considering the situation, I was surprised that my father was picking us up to take us to Grandma's. He said, keeping a straight face, "I have a surprise for you."

"Who me?"

He answered, "Yes." He guided us to my grandmother's front door. I was overjoyed to see that my grandfather, Richard, had returned from Korea.

Screaming in astonishment, "Papa," he hugged each of us tightly.

Our grandfather said, "Get your jacket and come on." After grabbing some refreshments, we set out. He surprised us with a drive-in movie, which astonished me since I had never done it before. I felt like I was at a Hollywood premiere. We saw The Karate Kid and Gremlins.

After arriving home late, we headed straight to bed. On Saturday, I got a later start to the day than usual. After waking up, I showered and ate breakfast. Although Jessie's remarks had entered my subconscious mind, I did not care because nothing would happen. Who was he to tell me I couldn't go to the park? My grandparents had gone out for breakfast, *so the park it is!*

I played Double Dutch with the other girls when I arrived at the park. I caught a glimpse of D approaching me, so I decided not to take my turn. D asked, "So, where's your little boyfriend?"

I replied, "What boyfriend?"

He continued, "Jessie, I know what it is! You were messing with him while you were messing with me."

"Jessie is my friend; I've never dated him."

D said, "I've got something for you to give him."

"I don't work for Pony Express; deliver it yourself."

He reached back from hamburger hill and slapped the he haw shit out of me. Before I knew it, I was on top of him, scratching, biting, and kicking. One of the neighbors ran down to get my grandma and grandpa, and when they arrived, I was still on top of him.

They pulled us apart, but not before I snatched off his glasses and said, "I got something for ya momma bitch! Another bill!" I broke those ugly glasses right in half. "I bet you didn't see that one coming, did you? Bitch."

Once we got back to my grandmother's house, the lecture began.

My Granddad remarked, "What has gotten into you, young woman?"

My aunt yelled across the room, "She's her mother's child!" I kept my head down and did not say anything for the next hour. My aunt's remark had left me feeling quite depressed. I'm not like my mother; that was an insult, just as she intended!

The neighbor came over to welcome my grandpa back. "Why is your head down, child?" he probed. When I told him I had gotten into a fight at the park, he said, "Well, you didn't do anything wrong," and added, "You were going about your day when he attacked you."

My grandfather responded, "Well, then, good job, tell these boys you didn't come to play."

The phone started ringing. When my aunt picked up the phone, she said, "Hey, kiddo. Jessie is on the phone." I sprang off the sofa like Tigger the Tiger; I couldn't wait to talk with Jessie.

I knew I was wrong, so I started with a disclaimer. It was almost like a confession. "Father, forgive me; I have sinned against thee," I said, "I know you said don't go down there, but I went to the park anyway." I began spilling the beans, telling him everything.

Jessie responded, "I knew he'd try something! I'm at my grandmother's place, and she's complaining about her minutes, so I'll talk to you on Monday. Oh, one more thing. STAY YO ASS AWAY FROM THE PARK!"

Chapter 12

After the Final Act Concludes; Then What?

Taking Jessie's advice to heart, I steered clear of the park all weekend. Monday morning came faster than a cheetah on roller skates. On the way to school, the boys kept chanting "Rocky vs. Drako" like a broken record. I knew that once we arrived, everyone would be chomping at the bit to get the scoop on what went down.

I was right. Maurice yelled as I crossed the street, "I'm going to beat his ass about my girl."

"Your girl?" I sassily responded as I burst out laughing.

Maurice replied while he rushed to catch up to me, wrapping his arm around my waist, "Come on, baby, stop playing; you know I look good on you!"

I shrieked and squirmed away, "Get off of me, dumbass!"

Out of nowhere, someone said, "Ya girl, hu," and everyone chuckled.

On the way to class, Jessie mentioned that I was the talk of the town. I replied, "I know; D has been talking about us like a dog." He said, "I'm glad you're okay, but the situation is far from over." "Just let it be," I urged.

Jessie replied, "He's talking too much, and I'm going to put a stop to that mouth."

"Now that I agree with, he's been acting like a little bird flying around dropping shit everywhere."

Jessie added, "He'd better keep my name out of his mouth. I told you not to go to the park, but I heard you won."

"I bet he won't ask me to deliver anything else," I said, and we both chuckled.

Despite Dad dropping us off at Grandma's the previous weekend, the dynamics of the relationship were unlike any I could remember. My father had found an apartment! He was determined not to move with her and insisted that his children didn't have to relocate out of state. Even though he had his own place, he consistently maintained control over our household, ensuring everything was in order. Every time we hopped into the car with him, he was always full of curiosity, asking us countless questions. It was always about what mom was up to, not how we were doing.

One day, I arrived home from school to find my mother laughing with her sisters on the phone. She responded, "Yeah, she just walked in.

Let me call y'all back."

"When your dad gets here, tell him you told me he tried to put his hand down your pants," she said.

I responded, "I didn't tell you that, and he didn't do that."

She said, "You better do what the fuck I said, or I'm going to teach you a lesson you won't forget."

I said, "I am not doing that because it didn't happen."

She grabbed my neck and yelled, "You heard what I said!" as I jerked away.

Well, as luck would have it, my dad walked in. She grudgingly informed him, "I gotta talk to you." He reluctantly agreed, and they made their way into the bedroom.

I heard him screaming, "Bitch stop lying. I know she didn't tell you anything like that; that didn't happen!" They began to fistfight.

Angrily, she yelled, "You tried to finger my daughter! I let it go the first time, but you had to try again. She's not lying; there's no reason for her to." Candice began to cry, and Kyle bolted for his room. Tears were streaming down my face while I sat on the couch.

I had yet to learn what this was about, why she was making up stories, and what she hoped to gain from it? I heard footsteps in the hallway. It was Dad. He yelled aggressively, "So, I tried to stick my hands down your pants?" I just stood there with tears streaming down my cheeks as I gazed at them both.

After a short while, my mother said, "Tell him what you told me!"

He continued, "I'm going to ask you one more time: did you tell your mom I tried to stick my hands in your pants?" I looked her in the eyes and nodded yes.

He said, "Man, you got to be shitting me; that is not true, and if it is, I apologize, but I do not recall anything like that happening."

And the Oscar goes to Jennie Mae, the cowardly lion! She burst into tears, yelling, "You sick bastard, you're just like your nasty ass daddy, and I'm done with you; you'll never see me or these kids again." That was her way out, and she took it. But at what cost?

You chose to be vindictive and lie instead of being woman enough to say, "Hey niggah, I'm done. Me and my kids are moving. If you don't want to go, you don't have to, but we're out of here."

Because of my anxiety, I thought it best to call it a night and retire early. I was feeling incredibly annoyed and exasperated. It was pretty disturbing to see my mother treating me in the same manner as those other predators. They were desperate for what I had and ready to do whatever it took to get it. This situation was far worse for me on so many levels. Her duty was to keep me safe and teach me right from wrong!

Unfortunately, everything I knew and felt was misguided. I continued to reflect on all that had transpired, weighing the various courses of action I could have chosen, but the truth was that I had lied. I wanted to call and apologize, but I was too scared of the consequences and how it would affect me going forward. Dad never returned to the house after that day, but we called him sometimes.

My mother went ahead with her relocation plans; she gave her notice and began packing our stuff. This was no longer something in my head but my new reality. What am I supposed to do? The next day, I mustered the courage to ask her when we would move. She began to say next week.

Wow, I wondered as I blurted out a million questions: "What about my Disney play?" I had been working hard on it, not to mention there were only two weeks left of school. "Why do we need to go right now? I want to do my part in the play. What about the newspaper?"

She screamed, "Shut up talking to me; you can't sing that good anyway." I walked away thinking, *Wait, what? So, you've beat me down, and now you're trying to tear me down with words; this can't be life.*

The following night at rehearsal, I informed my teacher immediately that I might not be able to perform in the play. When she questioned why, I explained that my mother told me we were moving. There was no time to find a replacement, so the school immediately called my mother and asked if she could bring me back for the last performance. She agreed to give it some thought.

My mother's words transformed into a ghost in the shadows. The next night at rehearsal, I began singing extremely low. "What's wrong?" the instructor asked, "Sing in your usual style."

My mother's words, "You can't sing that well anyway," were all I could hear. I explained that my throat hurts.

The play director jokingly pointed out, "Weren't you just having a casual chat with your pals a second ago? What in the world is going on here?" I had no choice but to tell her what my mother said. The director gasped for air and put her palm over her mouth. She said, "Your beautiful voice is why you were picked; you are gorgeous and perfect for the part." She took my hand and guided me toward the sound booth. She gave them the instructions to replay the rehearsal from yesterday.

We had yet to learn they were taping our rehearsals. I was astonished when she played it; I sounded fantastic; she hugged me and said,

"Block it out and go back to doing it your way because we love it."

What my mother said was water under the bridge, so I brushed it off and got to work! With the way I was nailing those notes, you'd have thought I was Whitney Houston in that bitch.

Jessie asked me whether my mother had told me I couldn't sing while he was walking me home; I nodded in agreement. "You can sing," he remarked, and "remember that!"

Once I got home, I showered, ate, and went to bed. That night, I prayed hard that something, anything, would happen so that I could do the play. Maybe missing the play was my payback for not telling the truth. I had rehearsed and was finally comfortable with the twirl, so I wanted to show off. If nothing else, I needed to prove to myself that I was capable of doing something right. My prayers had to have made it to God.

When I came home, I heard my mother running her mouth on the phone. I paused beside the door briefly just in case it revealed her mood. This time, it paid to listen. We were out of school on May 28th, and the place she thought she had needed more work than expected, so we would not be able to move until July. Yes, Lord, I will perform. She rolled her eyes at me when I walked in, but I didn't say a word.

As we strolled to school the following day, Jessie commented, "Damn, your mom looked mad when I knocked on the door this morning." I told him my mom was fuming because she got a call saying the apartment wouldn't be ready until July. Jessie said, "Oh, she going to be on you for real."

I said, "Screw her but listen, I am going over to my grandma's this weekend. We should try to collect the money from the paper route before people start receiving notifications about nonpayment." Jessie agreed. I began collecting as soon as we arrived at my grandmother's. A few customers inquired about the advance payment, but most handed over the money.

A time ago, while playing with my siblings, I accidentally kicked a hole in the wall. Fortunately, the bed hid it. The wall split so evenly that it looked more like a crack than a hole, and I cleverly used it to my benefit. Anything important was placed into the hole in the wall.

The night of the show was fast approaching. The newspaper was asked to come to the school to cover the performance for a feature. The piece quoted both Maurice and me. Maurice took advantage of every opportunity to sneak in a cheap feel during the photo shot. I was thrilled when the article was published. The school gave both Maurice and me a copy.

After the final bell rang, I couldn't wait to get home. My mother was not home when I arrived home, so I had a few moments of peace. I bounced around the kitchen, fresh-faced and grinning from ear to ear. I'm not sure which I savored more: the first spoonful of orange sherbert or the article; I enjoyed every minute of both! I read the piece nearly three times. I was scared my mother would destroy it, so I stashed the clipping in a small box inside the wall.

The moment of truth had arrived. Lights, camera action! I was on pins and needles, feeling a mix of nerves and excitement, but I was ready as could be! I had put a lot of effort into perfecting the dancing moves, using my right hand to grip, and hitting every line. The concert began promptly at seven. My father was absent, but my mother, siblings, aunts, uncles, and both sets of grandparents were in the building. I was having so much fun! Every detail was flawless.

In the last scene, I was meant to twirl and pretend to kiss Mickey, saying, "Oh Mickey, you're so pretty, don't you understand? You take me by the heart, not the lips." Maurice must have mistaken himself for the director and rewrote the damn script. After my twirl, he snatched me back to him and kissed me.

As I turned to face the crowd, I heard screams; they were coming from my mother. She jumped onto the stage and snatched me off the set, screaming, "I don't know what the fuck yall think this is but, I don't play that." I could not stop crying. I was so embarrassed. I knew the kids would make fun of me at school the next day.

When I returned to school the next day, I was met with only enthusiastic praise for my performance. My mother's climactic scene was cut at the very end. As a result, if you weren't there, it was just a myth, an urban legend. Fortunately, this was the play's final scene, the closing line. Otherwise, the entire production would have been doomed. I can't believe she made such a scene!

Maurice brought me a card and a dozen roses to class. He answered, "I had to give you something," he said. "Those lips followed me around in my sleep the entire night."

"You got me in trouble, punk," I replied, giving him a frog in his right arm.

He said, "I'm sorry, I didn't think she'd react that way." Tonae warned Maurice that she would lay his girlfriend out if she said anything to me as we headed to school.

Maurice said, "She's my ex-girlfriend. Do what you gotta do."

Tonae remarked, "Well, like I said, if she says anything about the play, she will be flat on the ground." I expected her to make fun of me.

However, the girl remained silent during class.

Now, when we went outside for recess, that was another story. Bringing two friends, she said, "How was that ass beating ya crazy ass mommy put on you?"

Tonae had me covered; she caught her with lefts and rights before I knew it. Tonae screamed, "I'm sick of you messing with my friend." The girl's defense mechanisms were a tad bit shabby; she tried to fight back but to no avail; she got her ass handed to her!

I screamed, "Uh huh, how was that ass-whooping my friend put on you?" When the teachers arrived, they broke up the fight. No one got in trouble since it was the final few days of classes. Which was a bonus.

I definitely enjoyed the free kicks to the ass.

The last day of school had arrived; the journey home seemed surreal. I was unsure if I would ever see them again. Every year on this day, we'd discuss how we would catch up during the summer. However, this year had a unique feel; it felt like the final curtain call, the last hurrah!

I felt like hiding under a rock and dying.

As we came closer to the house, I grieved quietly, tears streaming down my face. I wished Bianca were there to comfort me, but Jessie and Tonae were quick to step in. Tonae comforted me with a pat on the back as Jessie tried to console me with the words, "Don't cry. You know you'll see me; I only need an address."

I smiled and said, "Thank you," but I couldn't help but notice how everything that once brought me a sense of normalcy was undergoing a remarkable transformation right before my very eyes.

Jessie said, "I've got to tell you something, but don't get mad." I promised not to do so. He responded, "I went to D's school and fought him for fighting you."

I replied, "You're too late. Maurice already filled me in during one of our practices. I was waiting for you to say something. I heard you beat his ass again." I wanted to laugh, to find some humor in the situation, but the only response my body could muster was a torrent of tears.

With a grip firm on my shoulders, Jessie implored, 'Don't cry; we'll get through this, I promise!' After our heartfelt goodbyes, I retreated into the house.

When the 6 o'clock news came on, it showed a picture of Jessie's cousin and said he was being sought after for larceny. I quickly contacted Jessie, declaring, "Hey, your cousin is on the news,"

He replied, "Oh yeah, I was going to stop by and tell you tomorrow, but he is on the run for breaking into cars."

It was a perfect setup; the paper route company would easily believe he was the culprit. This scenario was not only plausible but also conveniently aligned with our intentions. Jessie responded, "The timing's spot on; it's a blessing in disguise. Don't fret; you're in the clear, you're moving, and you'll disappear without a trace." *Ironically, everything happens for a reason.*

I said, "Wow, we dodged a bullet. But what if he tells on you?" I asked.

He said, "Don't worry about me; it will never come back on you. That is all you need to worry about."

Jessie came by the next day to ask if I could talk to the farmers. I can't believe I worked so hard to get a deal for us and didn't reap any of the benefits. June saw a limited supply of berries in our neck of the woods, but the natural bounty came in July, August, and September. I explained to them that I would be moving and would no longer be able to assist them and that Jessie would hold down the fort.

As I expressed my gratitude to her, my head hung in despair, my chin formed an orange peel texture, and the corners of my mouth drew downward. Ms. Becky lifted my chin and said, "There's something else for you; don't be discouraged; everything will work out fine." I hugged her before walking away.

As the moving date approached, my withdrawal became more noticeable. My mother allowed me to go outside daily during the week we were meant to move. Tonae and I frequently discussed Bianca. The sudden disappearance of her family had us all puzzled and hoping for her safety. We had a blast sharing stories and reminiscing about the good old days from kindergarten to sixth grade. Despite how pleasant it felt, each evening seemed to bring us closer to the end.

The big day had arrived: moving day. Jessie came early and asked my mother if she wanted help loading boxes onto the truck. "Yes, I could use another set of hands," my mother remarked. Not only did our father not help us with the move, but he did not even stop by to wish us safe travels.

After loading the truck, Jessie said, "Come here for a minute." As we moved to the side, he continued, "I want you to know that no matter how far you think you are away, you're always close to my heart." "What if I never see you guys again?" I sobbed.

He replied, "That's not an option; my dad lives in that city, and there isn't enough space to keep us distant." Jessie embraced me and whispered gently, "I will miss you, sister. If you need any help, I am one phone call away. I can collect letters and deliver them to Tonae. Rest assured; everything will be fine."

I couldn't hold back my tears. I felt disheartened as our strong sibling bond seemed to be slipping away. Our creed was to be best friends forever; so much for that. It might have been easier if I had received further information regarding the individuals in the photograph alongside my biological father. However, those answers remained locked away in the river, just like my mother's heart!

My cousins were overjoyed about the move; that was all they talked about. However, my excitement was dampened by what I might lose. *How am I going to make money? Will I meet new friends?* I couldn't help but wonder if I would be relocating to a different state, where a whole new set of predators awaited me. I pondered whether I could safeguard myself from these potential dangers.

Ambiguity left me feeling vulnerable and unsafe. From the little girl standing at the casket of a nameless man who had suddenly become my father, making the only family members I knew feel like present strangers. Deep within, there were scars from all of the hurt and pain.

I had the feeling that disaster was just around the corner. I didn't know what was behind anything anymore. The only thing I was certain of was that everything was uncertain. I couldn't help but ponder the eternal query, *who in the world am I?* I did not know what lay ahead, but I did know one thing: I would be the captain of my fate. In a bold move, I decided to embrace the philosophy of "right is right, and wrong is still fucking wrong." My mission? To ensure that everyone I crossed paths with would fully comprehend this concept from here on out.

I was not going to let anything, or anyone control me. I trembled with fear at the thought of leaving behind what I knew, but rest assured; if shit got funky, I was fully prepared to engage in some serious posterior pummeling and postpone the identification process. In other words, I was going to beat ass and take names later.

Then, like a lightning bolt slicing through the midnight sky, the 'Aha!' moment struck. It was not just an awakening but a revelation, a seismic shift in my understanding of the world. I realized the profound significance of names and their power; the power to shape our identities, destinies, and very existence. Allow me to introduce myself: I am Destiny Sampson, not just Destiny Sampson, but Destiny Sampson, unique and unparalleled. I am not a puppet dancing to the whims of chance; I am the master of my outcome. Move aside, fate! I'm taking the wheel of my destiny. There's only one blockbuster story in town, and guess what? It's debuting yours truly!

Don't miss out!

Stay in the loop with Elunda Sanders' latest publications by signing up for our free email updates. Visit the website below, and you'll never miss a new release from this author. Remember, there's no obligation - just an excellent opportunity to learn about Elunda Sanders' latest books.

https://books2read.com/r/B-A-UWPJB-ZFQED

BOOKS 2 READ

Connecting independent readers to independent writers.

About the Author

Elunda Sanders is a woman who possesses a wide range of talents. She effortlessly juggles the roles of nurse, sister, friend, mother of four, and now author. Her eight grandchildren fill her days with boundless joy and serve as her daily motivation. Elunda thoroughly enjoys exploring new places and making meaningful connections with people, thanks to her charming personality and captivating smile. She lives at the crossroads of belief and imagination. Nursing is her primary passion, but writing has become an additional channel for her to share her wisdom and stories. Above all, Elunda's utmost devotion lies with God, who she believes directs her journey and grants her a sense of meaning.